Time Will Darken It one fe
and place and time—ha
rendered." Eudora Welty concurred: "Mr. Maxwell's public is well aware that his sensitive prose is the good and careful tool of an artist who is always doing exactly what he means to do." His next book, *Stories* (1956), features some of Maxwell's early short fiction along with work by Jean Stafford and John Cheever.

Maxwell turned to a very different theme in *The Château* (1961), a novel that traces the experiences, both exhilarating and confusing, of an American couple, tourists, who fall in love with France in 1948. *"The Château . . .* is a large-scale work whose smallest details are beautifully made," wrote Naomi Bliven. "This novel is fiction with the authenticity of a verified document, a history of what some citizens of the splintered Western World might say or mean to each other in our period." In 1966 Maxwell brought out *The Old Man at the Railroad Crossing and Other Tales,* a collection of fables in which he mixes the traditions of Aesop, the Brothers Grimm, and Kafka. "Mr. Maxwell's morals and proverbs are always original, frequently funny, and often ironic and profound," said *The New York Times Book Review.*

Maxwell ventured into nonfiction with *Ancestors* (1971), an entrancing history of his forebears. "Maxwell's uncommon family history is an exploration of the past in which the novelist's invention figures as large as the historian's research," stated *The New York Times Book Review.* "It is notable for its quiet humor, affectionate tone, and sharp vision of another America." His next book, *Over by the River and Other Stories* (1977), comprises work he published over a period of thirty years in *The New Yorker.* "Maxwell's gifts as a writer allow him to impose upon his material a gentle, rather Chekhovian sense of order," observed Joyce Carol Oates. "Whatever happens is not Fate but the inevitable working-out of character, never melodramatic, never pointedly 'symbolic.'"

So Long, See You Tomorrow earned Maxwell the American Book Award in 1980. Though the central event of this novel is a murder that actually occurred on an Illinois farm in the early 1920s, the book is also an astonishingly inventive memoir of childhood. "In this splendid novel William Maxwell attains his highest power," said novelist Shirley Hazzard. "The inexorable Middle Western setting and the fated passions of his characters are realizations of the most thrilling literary quality. In a deeply American book I was reminded over and over of the great Russian writers."

The Outermost Dream, a compilation of Maxwell's essays and reviews originally published in *The New Yorker,* appeared in 1989. Many of the pieces focus on the diaries, biographies, and memories of such writers as Colette, E. M. Forster, and Virginia Woolf. "In this one wonderful volume, we get Mr. Maxwell's clear prose, his magical narrative, and the attractions of his quirky mind," said *The New York Times Book Review.*

Maxwell's most recent fiction continues to earn critical acclaim. In *Billie Dyer and Other Stories* (1992), Maxwell revisits his native town of Lincoln, Illinois, in the early 1900s and considers some of its inhabitants who have remained haunting figures to him. "These new stories of William Maxwell's achieve their greatness invisibly," wrote Reynolds Price. "Like their peers in the work of Tolstoy, Chekhov, Porter, and Welty, they slowly lure the reader into ironclad but transparent rooms. And soon we're held in the arms of a huge benign host who wills us only an elegant pleasure, a deepened vision of our lost past, and a comprehending mercy now, in the smaller world of our diminished present." *All the Days and Nights* (1995), his latest collection of stories, makes it clear why critic Bruce Bawer wrote, "Mr. Maxwell is blessed with a rare sense of wonder: his books constantly remind us that life, love, friendship, youth, and a sense of beauty are mysterious gifts, things to marvel at."

In 1989 the poet Howard Moss paid Maxwell this tribute: "By the time his second novel, *They Came Like Swallows*, appeared in 1937, it was clear that William Maxwell was a special and wonderful gift to American fiction. It may be the definitive American novel about a child's relationship to his mother—a subject so obvious, and crucial, that it is rarely handled. Similarly, *The Folded Leaf* became a classic study of adolescent relationships—two boys, and then a girl—the web so delicately and truthfully examined that the book continues to be a revelation for succeeding generations. *The Château* harked back to James in its subject of Americans abroad, and in its probing of moral inscrutabilities it can stand comparison to the Master. Best of all, probably, is Maxwell's most recent novel, *So Long, See You Tomorrow*, the story of a murder in the twenties and its effect on the friendship of two thirteen-year-old boys. The Middle West, especially in *Time Will Darken It*, is Maxwell's particular territory, but he is as knowing and skillful about life in New York and France as well. As for life in general, one need merely read him. The least flashy of writers, a writer's writer, he is controlled and reserved, and yet magical at the same time. He has been a master of fiction for almost fifty years."

Introduction

An English instructor at the University of Illinois, who was my mentor during all four years of college, had a sabbatical some time about the year 1930 and went around the world. I don't know in what country he picked up a copy of the Tauschnitz edition of *To the Lighthouse*. Shortly after he got home he offered it to me, saying, "I couldn't read this but you may like it." His idea of the perfect novel was Fielding's *Tom Jones*. I perhaps don't need to explain that the central figure of *To the Lighthouse*, Mrs. Ramsay, is a woman who, by her protecting nature and desire for harmony, is able to reconcile, briefly, and only to a certain extent, the clashing temperaments of her husband and children and of the guests who have been invited to stay with the Ramsays in their house on the coast of Cornwall. On the very first page I came upon my doppelgänger:

> Since he belonged, even at the age of six, to that great clan which cannot keep this feeling separate from that, but must let future prospects, with their joys and sorrows, cloud what is ac-

tually at hand, since to such people even in earliest childhood any turn in the wheel of sensation has the power to crystallise and transfix the moment upon which its gloom or radiance rest, James Ramsay, sitting on the floor cutting out pictures from the illustrated catalogue of the Army and Navy Stores, endowed the picture of a refrigerator, as his mother spoke, with heavenly bliss.

My mother's death, in the epidemic of Spanish influenza of 1918, so scarred my soul that I would, I am sure, have written about it sooner or later but in any case the way I did write about it was strongly affected by the style and narrative method of *To the Lighthouse.* Saul Bellow, speaking at a literary symposium at Smith College in the fifties, said, "A writer is a reader who is moved to emulation." I took it that he did not mean mere copying. Mrs. Woolf was strongly affected by reading Proust. ("Oh if I could write like that!" she said. And decided that she could. And discovered she couldn't.) In the paragraph I have quoted there is an echo of his syntax.

I saw in Mrs. Ramsay a woman rather like my mother, who was acutely responsive to other people's happiness or distress, whose voice I associate with velvet, who lived by the pure feelings of the heart. That this reflects a child's point of view is obvious. Because Virginia Woolf disposed of Mrs. Ramsay's death in a brief, terrible parenthesis, leaving the reader in ignorance of what led up to it, I felt my hands were not tied. I could go where she had chosen not to.

If you toss a small stone into a pond, it will create a ripple that expands outward, wider and wider. And if you then toss a second stone, it will again produce a widening circle inside the first one. And with the third stone there will be three expanding concentric circles before the pond recovers its stillness through the force of gravity. That is what I wanted my novel to be like. No directions came with this idea. I have tried to recall, across the intervening sixty years, how I went about writing *They Came Like Swallows* and what I remember instead is the places I wrote in.

When I was seventeen I had a summer job on a farm near Portage, Wisconsin, and it became a second home. Middlewestern farms do not usually offer much pleasure to the eye but this one did. Besides a log house and a frame house that was much older, there was a horse barn and the usual outbuildings, a forty-acre stand of oak trees, hay meadows, and a marsh with a small swift-running stream meandering through it. The banks were lined with wild rice, which in the fall Indians harvested from their canoes. What was originally a water tower had been converted into a three-story frame building. On the first floor there was a single room with a grand piano. Josef Lhévinne, the great Russian pianist, was a friend of the family and came to the farm at least once during every summer. The piano was for him to use when he was preparing for a season of concertizing. On my hands and knees in the vegetable garden, pulling weeds, I would hear the beginning notes of the Chopin A Minor Étude, Opus 25, and straighten up to listen: In the upper half of the keyboard, musical fireworks. In the lower half, the imperturbable melodic line. The second floor of the tower was his bedroom. The third floor, reached by an outside stairway, was a little study with a brick fireplace, white wicker furniture covered with a cheerful cretonne, and a desk facing a window. I went there once at the end of winter and found, between the cushions of the chaise longue, the dry odorless body of a dead squirrel. It had come down the chimney, been unable to get up it again, and died there of hunger and cold. If I had understood and allowed myself to feel the full implications of this lonely death I would have become, in that instant, a mature novelist.

When I began to write seriously, this room among the treetops was turned over to me. I forget how many months I sat in that room, at that little desk, struggling. I needed to forget Virginia Woolf and establish contact with a figure out of antiquity—the old, often blind, professional storyteller who made his living by standing on the riverbank by the ferry landing or by some crossroads, telling tales that began "Once upon a time there was a . . ." As I searched for the form I believed was implicit in the material, I would hear the crows bad-mouthing one another. A goldfinch or a robin would settle on the branch outside my window and then fly off. Sometimes I stopped typing in order to enjoy a summer thunderstorm. I tried telling the story in the first person and in the third. Neither one worked. The omniscient author knew too much and at the same time too little. I did seven versions of Part One, each about a hundred pages long, and wasn't satisfied with any of them.

The summer of 1935 I had a fellowship to the MacDowell Colony. There I was given a fieldstone studio to write in, with a desk and a typewriter, a table and some chairs, a fireplace and plenty of logs to burn in it. I slept in the men's dormitory. At noon a picnic basket containing my lunch was left on the doorstep of my studio and usually I was sitting there waiting for it. In the afternoon I went walking. The air of southern New Hampshire is fresh and smells of pine needles. I would stand and watch huge cloud formations turn on some invisible axis and in an instant become deep blue sky. Sometimes I walked in the woods, sometimes I went downhill into the village of Peterborough, where I stepped into the bookstore or walked up one street and down the next admiring the old houses. In a grove of trees in the center of town I discovered a pond large enough to swim in and quite deserted. After that, when I went walking I usually took my swimming trunks with me. Many years later, I learned that the hours I kept were the subject of amused comment by the other colonists, who spent the whole day working in their studios, but my judgment failed along about twelve-thirty and after that there was no point in my sitting in front of a typewriter.

Among the colonists that summer there were only three with any conspicuous talent—the surrealist painter Louis Guglielmi, who died young; the composer David Diamond, who was only seventeen; and the poet and translator Robert Fitzgerald. About the others the most you could say was that they were pleasant company. Among them was a Brazilian composer who was writing a triple fugue, a woman who was doing her Ph.D. thesis on the last ten years of Wordsworth's life, during which he wrote nothing of any consequence, and a poet whose copy of Elinor Wylie's *Angels and Earthly Creatures* had been plagiarized from so often that the pages were coming unsewed. The Brazilian composer was carrying on an extensive correspondence with orchestra managers all over the world and enlisted my help, his English not being up to it. From time to time I rebelled and then he would sit down at the piano and play Busoni's transcription of the Bach chaconne, after which I would go on turning his pidgin English into something more businesslike. A painter named Charlotte Blass needed a model and I sat for her. Husbands, wives, friends, lovers came and went. The bachelors complained of sexual impotence and suspected Mrs. MacDowell of putting saltpeter in the coffee. Diamond saw Elinor Wylie's ghost. It struck me that living in an artists' colony was a little like sleeping six in a bed.

Fitzgerald grew up in Springfield, Illinois, thirty miles from where I was living most of that time. We became friends during the year I spent as a graduate student at Harvard. He was two years younger and much better educated. His mother died when he was three, his younger brother when he was seven. And while he was away at boarding school, a year or two before I met him, his father, whom he worshipped, died of tuberculosis of the bone. I learned far more about literature from him than I did from my encounters with the English faculty at Harvard. Except for a brief bad period in my sophomore year, my college days had been happy and I was cheerfully skittering around on the surface of things. Fitzgerald loathed the undemanding, the mindless, the merely charming, and he took me, almost literally, by the scruff of the neck and forced me to recognize the tragic nature of life. That summer at the MacDowell Colony he was collaborating with Dudley Fitts on a verse translation of the *Alcestis* of Euripides. In this play the heroine dies and is brought back to life through the intervention of Hercules. Without the help of Hercules I was trying to do much the same thing. Fitzgerald's room at the colony was directly above mine and I used to listen attentively to the sound of his footsteps climbing the outside stairway or pacing back and forth across the ceiling. His very presence was a help to me. I managed to break through, finally, into a kind of narrative that didn't deliquesce by the following morning.

—

On the first of September his stay expired and he left to spend a few weeks in the house of a relative in Annapolis.

Mine, God knows why, had been extended to the end of the month. During that time I finished an eighth version of Part One, that I felt would stand, and began Part Two.

It had been agreed that on my way home to Illinois, at the beginning of October, I would stop off and see Fitzgerald in Annapolis, and that he would meet me in the train station in Baltimore, but when I stepped down from the train I didn't see him. It took me a minute or two to accept the fact that he wasn't anywhere, and I didn't have his telephone number. I waited around for an hour and then took the trolley to Annapolis. It was night by the time I got there. I gave a taxi driver the address, in Epping Forest, which I took to be a development but it turned out to be a real forest, full of cottages that were boarded up for the winter. We drove round and round in the dark peering at street signs and finally saw a house with a lighted window. While he waited with his motor running, I knocked on the door and a middle-aged woman opened it. "Oh, yes," she said. "I know where Miss Stuart's house is, and I could show it to you from where we are standing if it were daytime, but I don't think I can tell you how to get there. . . . Come in. . . . My niece has gone to the movies. When she gets home she'll take you there."

I paid the driver and sat down in a straight chair with my suitcase beside me. It had been a long day. I wondered if something had happened to Fitzgerald—like a car accident. I thought how trusting people were in the South. I glanced at my wristwatch. It was still early. The woman said, "I can see you are tired. Why don't you go to bed in my niece's room, and I'll wait up for her." So I did. And woke to bright sunlight, and dressed, and the woman, whose name I told myself I would remember all the days of my life but that I have nevertheless forgotten, gave me toast and coffee and pointed out the house, across a small ravine, where Fitzgerald would be staying.

He didn't appear to find it remarkable that I had managed to make my way to where he was.

"I meant to come and meet you," he said, holding the screen door open. We sat down at a table and I watched his face for signs of approval or disapproval as he read the chapter about Robert and his friends playing football.

———

I settled down in Urbana, Illinois, in the house of a retired banker, whose daughter, Garreta Busey, was a member of the English Department and also my friend. The arrangement we made was that in exchange for room and board and four dollars a month I would read her examination papers, which she said she could no longer bear the sight of. I suspect that she wanted to help me get on with my novel and chose this tactful way to go about it.

There was nearly always a student or two living in the house. In the past I had been one of them. It stood on half a block of ground and had the settled, softened look that old places tend to have. There was a violet bed by the front walk, and a cucumber tree had grown one very long limb protectively around the side porch. The downstairs woodwork was of cherry. The rooms were well lighted and of such generous proportions that it seemed a privilege to walk through them. I think it unlikely that anyone ever lived there who didn't appreciate its meditative stillness. Including the arsonist who, a dozen years ago, poured gasoline here and there and burned the place to the ground. I had a large bedroom and an adjoining room to write in, with only one window, which looked out on a section of tin roof so lacking in interest that after a brief glance I turned back to the typewriter. On a good day I managed to do a page that didn't end up in the wastebasket. Objects— Bunny's yellow agate, Robert's toy soldiers, the clocks that could not agree about what time it was—even though they didn't exist anymore were at my disposal. Turning an actual person into a character in a novel was more tricky. Facts alone did not supply them with the breath of life. I had to believe myself in their created existence.

I have dealt, in one partly autobiographical novel or another and in short stories, with the disaster that overtook our family in the year 1918. Because I was only ten at the time of my mother's death, there were things I didn't know or that were kept from me. I think that in the end I got all the circumstances right. But I am not sure that these later retellings are as affecting as the first one, where I made myself two years younger than I actually was, played ducks and drakes with chronology, gave one person's experience to another, introduced domestic habits from households I came to know later, and freely mixed fact with fiction. It may be simply that when I was writing *They Came Like Swallows* the heartbreaking actual events had not yet receded into the past.

It took all winter to finish Part Two. I wrote Part Three in ten days. Much of the time I walked the floor, framing sentences in my mind and then brushing the tears away with my hand so I could see the typewriter keys. I was weeping, I think, both for what happened—for I could not write about my mother's death without reliving it—and for events that took place only in my imagination. I don't suppose I was entirely sane.

They came like swallows and like swallows went,
And yet a woman's powerful character
Could keep a swallow to its first intent;
And half a dozen in formation there,
That seemed to whirl upon a compass-point,
Found certainty upon the dreaming air . . .

W. B. YEATS

CONTENTS

BOOK ONE

WHOSE
ANGEL CHILD

I

Bunny did not waken all at once. A sound (what, he did not know) struck the surface of his sleep and sank like a stone. His dream subsided, leaving him awake, stranded, on his bed. He turned helplessly and confronted the ceiling. A pipe had burst during the winter before, and now there was the outline of a yellow lake. The lake became a bird with a plumed head and straggling tail feathers, while Bunny was looking at it. When there were no further changes, his eyes wandered down by way of the blue-and-white wallpaper to the other bed, where Robert lay sleeping. They lingered for a moment upon Robert's parted lips, upon his face drained and empty with sleep.

It was raining.

Outside, branches of the linden rose and fell in the wind, rose and fell. And November leaves came down. Bunny turned over upon the small unyielding body of Araminta Culpepper. Because he was eight, and somewhat past the age when boys are supposed to play with dolls, Araminta hung from the bedpost by day—an Indian papoose with an unbreakable expression on her face. But at night she shared his bed with him. A dozen times he drew her to him lovingly in sleep. And if he woke too soon, the darkness was neither frightful nor bare so long as he could put out his hand and touch her.

Before him—before Peter Morison who was called Bunny—was the whole of the second Sunday in November, 1918. He moved slightly in order that Araminta Culpepper might have room for her head on the pillow. If it had been a clear day, if the sky were blue and full of sunlight, he would have to go off to Sunday school and sing hymns and perhaps hear the same old story about Daniel who was put in the lions' den, or about Elisha, or about Elijah who went to heaven in a chariot of fire. And what would become of his morning? As soon as he got home and spread the funny-paper out on the floor where he could look at it comfortably, some one would be sure to come along and exclaim over him: *For Heaven's sake, it's too nice a day to be in the house. Why don't you go outdoors and get some exercise?* And if he pretended that he was going to but didn't, they would come again in a little while. He would have to put on his cap and his woolly coat and mittens, whether he wanted to or not. He would be driven out of the house to roll disconsolately in a bed of leaves or to wander through the garden where nothing bloomed; where there were only sticks and crisp grass and the stalks of summer flowers.

But not now, Bunny said to himself, hearing the sound of water dripping, dropping from the roof. Not this morning. And somewhere in the front part of the house a door opened so that his mother's voice came up the stairs. A spring inside him, a coiled spring, was set free. He sat up and threw his covers to the foot of the bed. When he was washed and dressed he went downstairs. His mother was sitting at the breakfast table before the fire in the library.

"How do you do?" He threw his arms about her and planted a kiss somewhat wildly on her mouth. "How do you do and how do you do again?"

"I do very well, thank you."

She held him off in front of her to see whether he had washed thoroughly, and Bunny noticed with relief the crumbs at his father's place, the carelessly folded napkin.

"Did you have a good night? Is Robert up?"

Bunny shook his head.

"Stirring?"

"No."

"I thought that would happen."

While Bunny settled himself at the table she buttered a piece of toast for him. He was old enough to butter his own but she liked doing it for him. She was that way. When she had finished she lifted the platter of bacon from the hearth.

"Robert stayed up until ten o'clock, trying to finish *The Boy Allies in Bulgaria*. I told him they wouldn't assassinate anybody without him, but he wanted to finish it just the same." She helped herself to another cup of coffee. "You know how he is."

Robert was thirteen and very trying. More so, it seemed to Bunny, than most people. He wouldn't go to bed and he wouldn't get up. He hated to bathe or be kissed or practise his music lesson. He left the light burning in the basement. He refused to eat oysters or squash. He wouldn't get up on cold mornings and close the window. He spread his soldiers all over the carpet in the living-room and when it came time to pick them up he was never there; he had gone off to help somebody dig a cave. And likely as not he would come home late for dinner, his clothes covered with mud, his knuckles skinned, his hair full of leaves and sticks, and a hole in his brand-new sweater.

There was no time (no time that Bunny could remember) when Robert had not made him cry at least once between morning and night. Robert hid Bunny's thrift stamps and his ball of lead foil. Or he danced through the house swinging Araminta Culpepper by the braids. Or he twisted Bunny's arm and showed him a fine new trick, the point of which was that he got his thumbs bent out of shape. Or he might do no more than sit across the room saying, *Creepy-creepy-creepy* . . . pointing his finger at Bunny and describing smaller and smaller circles until the tears would not stay back any longer.

Before this day was over, it too would be spoiled like all the others. But while Robert was still upstairs in bed there was nothing for Bunny to worry about, no reason on earth why he should not enjoy his breakfast.

"It's raining," he said, and helped himself to bacon.

"I see it is." His mother took the plate from him and put it back on the hearth to keep warm for Robert. "It's been raining since five o'clock."

Bunny looked out of the window hopefully.

"Hard?"

Sometimes when it rained heavily for a considerable time he was not expected to go outside even though it cleared up afterward. The ground was too wet, they said. He might catch his death.

"Hard, Muv?"

"Like this."

Bunny tried to persuade himself that it was a heavy rain, but there was too much wind and not enough water. All the whirling and criss-crossing, the beating against the window and sliding in sudden rivulets down the glass—there was very little to it. The wind rose higher and the rain turned itself about and about. The room became intensely still, so that logs crackling and singing in the fireplace seemed loud and impressive. And because the lights were on in the daytime, the walls seemed immensely substantial, the way they did at night with curtains drawn across the windows and the room closed in upon itself.

"Do you think, Muv——"

Bunny hesitated, fearing at the last moment to expose himself.

"Rain before seven——"

His mother got up from the table, having read his thought, and answered it, severely:

Rain before seven
Clear by eleven.

Bunny was obliged to unwind the proverb in his own mind. There was nothing else for him to do. The words she had left unspoken remained cruelly before his eyes even when he looked down at his plate. With great concentration he began to eat his cereal. It would have taken a very little thing at that moment to spill his sorrow. Let the clock catch its breath, let one log fall with a sudden shower of sparks up the chimney and he would have wept.

His mother sat down in the window seat and hunted through her sewing-kit impatiently. Bunny could hear her saying to herself that he was a grown man, or nearly so. Eight last August and not yet able to depend on his own strength, but coming to her again and again to be reassured.

Another time, he promised; another time he would try and not give in to weakness. If only she would not be severe with him now. He could not bear to have her that way. Not this morning. . . . Feeling altogether sorry for himself, he began to imagine what it would be like if she were not there. If his mother were not there to protect him from whatever was unpleasant—from the weather and from Robert and from his father—what would he do? Whatever would become of him in a world where there was neither warmth nor comfort nor love?

Rain washed against the window.

When his mother found the needle she had been looking for, she threaded it. Then she took up a square of white cloth. Her hand flew this way and that, over her sewing. Quite suddenly she spoke to him:

"Bunny, come here."

He got down from his chair at once. But while he stood waiting before her and while she considered him with eyes that were perplexed and brown, the weight grew. The weight grew and became like a stone. He had to lift it each time that he took a breath.

"Whose angel child are you?"

By these words and by the wholly unexpected kiss that accompanied them he was made sound and strong. His eyes met hers safely. With wings beating above him and a great noise as of trumpets and drums he returned to his breakfast.

II

What are you making? tea towels?"

Bunny noticed that his mother had a very curious way of shaking her head. Rather as if she were shaking away an idea that buzzed.

"They *do* look like tea towels."

The interest which he took in her affairs was practically contemporary. If she were invited to a card party he wanted to know afterward who won the prize, and what they had to eat, and what the place cards were like. When she went to Peoria to shop he liked to be taken along so that he could pass judgment on her clothes, though it meant waiting for periods of time outside the fitting-room. Nor did they always agree. About the paper in the dining-room, for instance. Bunny thought it quite nice the way it was. Especially the border, which was a hill with the same castle on it every three feet. And the same three knights riding up to each of the castles. Nevertheless, his mother had it done over in plain paper that gave him nothing to think about, and might far better, in his opinion, have been used for the kitchen, where it wouldn't so much matter.

"If they aren't tea towels, what are they?"

He waited impatiently while she bit off the thread and measured a new length from her spool.

"Diapers."

The word started a faint spinning of excitement within him. He went thoughtfully and sat down beside his mother in the window seat. From there he could see the side yard and the fence, Koenig's yard, and the side of Koenig's white house. The Koenigs' were German but they couldn't help that, and they had a little girl whose name was Anna. In January Anna would be a year old. Mr. Koenig got up very early to help with the washing before he went to work. The washing-machine galumpty-lumped, galumpty-lumped, at five o'clock in the morning. By breakfast time there would be a string of white flags blowing in the autumn wind. They weren't flags, of course; they were diapers. And that was just it. People never made diapers unless somebody was going to have a baby.

Bunny listened. For a moment he was outside in the rain. He was wet and shining. His mind bent from the wind. He detached a wet leaf. But one did not speak of these things.

Always when he and his mother were alone, the library seemed intimate and familiar. They did not speak or even raise their eyes, except occasionally. Yet around and through what they were doing each of them was aware of the other's presence. If his mother were not there, if she was upstairs in her room or out in the kitchen explaining to Sophie about lunch, nothing was real to Bunny—or alive. The vermilion leaves and yellow leaves folding and unfolding upon the curtains depended utterly upon his mother. Without her they had no movement and no color.

Now, sitting in the window seat beside her, Bunny was equally dependent. All the lines and surfaces of the room bent toward his mother, so that when he looked at the pattern of the rug he saw it necessarily in relation to the toe of her shoe. And in a way he was more dependent upon her presence than the leaves or flowers. For it was the nature of his possessions that they could be what they actually were, and also at certain times they could turn into knights and crusaders, or airplanes, or elephants in a procession. If his mother went downtown to cut bandages for the Red Cross (so that when he came home from school he was obliged to play by himself) he could never be sure that the transformation would take place. He might push his marbles around the devious and abrupt pattern of the Oriental rug for hours, and they would never be anything but marbles. He put his hand into the bag now and drew out a yellow agate which became King Albert of Belgium.

A familiar *thump* brought him somewhat painfully again into the world of the library. *Thump thump thump*—all the way across the ceiling. Robert was getting up.

"I've been thinking."

Bunny looked down in time to see his mother's hand spread over his and inclose it.

"About the back room. I told Robert he could have a bed in there, and some chairs, and fix it up the way he likes. He's getting old enough now so that he likes to be by himself."

Bunny nodded. Sometimes when he and his mother were alone they discussed Robert in this way, and what should be done about him.

"If we do that, of course, there won't be anybody to stay with you."

He liked to have her bend down and brush the top of his head lightly with her cheek. But he would have preferred another time. Now it confused him. He turned his eyes toward the window and the damp trees, toward the rain-drenched ground. As soon as the window was clear enough for him to see through, a fresh gust drove against it from the other side and everything blurred. It was that way when his mother kissed him. This talk about moving Robert into the back room where his Belgian city was, where he kept his magic lantern. What had that to do with *diapers*?

"You see——" His mother spread the white cloth over her knees, folded it, laid it with the others in a pile. "What we need is another person in the family. At least one other person."

"I think we're getting along quite well the way things are."

"Perhaps. But the room you're in. It's ever so much too——"

Her hand opened and lay still.

Some one to fill up his room. Like the Mr. Crumb that stayed at Miss Brew's, three houses down on the same side of the street.

"We're not going to take in roomers, are we?"

"No, not roomers, exactly. I wouldn't like that."

"I wouldn't, either!"

Mr. Crumb had such a large nose. It would be upsetting to wake and find him in Robert's bed early in the morning.

"What I had in mind was something that bordered on a small brother or a small sister—it wouldn't matter which, would it? So you wouldn't rattle around in there the way you do when you are all alone."

"No, I suppose not. But does that mean———"

He had seen her stop sometimes on her way upstairs, to catch her breath at the landing. It was that way now. And though she smiled reassuringly, her eyes were darker than he had ever known them to be.

"Muv, does that mean we're going to have to have a baby here?"

"All things considered, I think it does."

But that was too much. Bunny sat absolutely still, watching the yellow leaves contract; watching the spider swing itself out upon the ceiling.

III

Although the library had been familiar at breakfast time, Bunny knew that it was now subject to change, to uncertainty. His father had come home again and would be home, said the big clock in the hall, for the day.... The little brass clock emerged out of a general silence, asserting that it was not so; that Mr. Morison would go out again after dinner. . . . They argued, then. The grandfather's clock made slow involved statements which the other replied to, briefly. "Quarter of ten," said the grandfather's clock, untroubled by the irrelevance. "Ten till," said the little brass clock on the mantel. So long as that went on, Bunny could not be sure of anything.

His father had settled himself on the chaise-longue, with the Sunday paper. From time to time he solemnly turned the pages. When he read aloud he expected everybody to listen.

"*What is Spanish influenza?... Is it something new?... Does it come from Spain?... The disease now occurring in this country and called 'Spanish influenza' resembles a very contagious kind of 'cold' accompanied by fever, pains in the head, eyes, back, or other parts of the body, and a feeling of severe sickness. In most of the cases the symptoms disappear after three or four days, the patient rapidly recovering. Some of the patients, however, develop pneumonia, or inflammation of the ear, or meningitis, and many of these complicated cases die. Whether this so-called 'Spanish influenza' is identical with the epidemic of earlier years is not known. . . ."*

The word epidemic was new to Bunny. In his mind he saw it, unpleasantly shaped and rather like a bed pan.

". . . Although the present epidemic is called 'Spanish influenza,' there is no reason to believe that it originated in Spain. Some writers who have studied the question believe that the epidemic came from the Orient and they call attention to the fact that the Germans mention the disease as occurring along the eastern front in the summer and fall of 1917."

By the calm way that his father crossed one knee over the other it was clear that he was concerned with the epidemic—but only of his own free will, because he chose to be concerned with such things.

When Bunny was very small he used to wake in the night sometimes with a parched throat and call for a drink of water. It was one of the few things that worked invariably. He heard stumbling and lurching, and the sound of water running in the bathroom. The side of a glass struck his teeth. He drank thirstily and fell back into sleep. . . . Until one night across the intervening darkness a voice said, *Oh, get it yourself!* For the first time in his life Bunny was made aware of the fact that he had a father. And thoroughly shocked, he did as he was told.

Ever since that time he had been trying to make a place for his father within his own arranged existence—and always unsuccessfully. His father was not the kind of man who could be fit into anybody's arrangement except his own. He was too big, for one thing. His voice was too loud. He was too broad in the shoulder, and he smelled of cigars. In the family orchestra his father played the piano, Robert the snare drum, Bunny the bass drum and cymbals. His father started the music going with his arms, with his head. And in no time at all the sound was tremendous—filling the open center of the room, occupying the space in corners and behind chairs.

"*. . . In contrast to the outbursts of ordinary coughs and colds, which usually occur in the cold months, epidemics of influenza may occur at any season of the year, thus the present epidemic raged most intensely in Europe in May, June, and July. Moreover, in the case of ordinary colds, the general symptoms (fever, pain, depression) are by no means so severe . . .*"

Bunny saw that his mother was threatened with a sneeze. She closed her eyes resignedly and waited.

"*. . . or as sudden in their outset as they are in influenza. Finally, ordinary colds do not spread through the community so rapidly or so extensively as does influenza. . . .*"

Watching his mother, Bunny felt an acute though momentary suspension within his own brain. His nose tickled. He pressed one finger against his upper lip. When his mother rolled her eyes at him, conveying the information that her misery was boundless, Bunny turned to his father. How was it that his father did not know? that he could go on reading?

"*Ordinarily the fever lasts from three to four days and the patient recovers. . . . As in other catching diseases, a person who has only a mild attack of the disease may give a very severe attack to others. . . .*"

The sneeze came. His mother's composure was destroyed by it. She fumbled for her handkerchief.

"... *When death occurs it is usually the result of a complication.*"

"James——"

"Yes?"

"Do you mind?"

"Mind what?"

"If it's all the same, I wish you'd read about something else—floods in China, or the Kaiser. Already I've begun to have fever, pains, and depression."

"If it will make you any happier."

The largest and the smallest of Bunny's agates raced along a red strip in the pattern of the library rug. After their discussion at breakfast, Bunny had hoped that his mother would come around to his way of thinking—that it was neither wise nor necessary to take on a baby at this time. Later, perhaps.... Remembering the wall paper in the dining-room he felt sure that she would go ahead with her plans. His mother and he were getting along well enough the way things were. That was his point. And of course there would be sewing. From what he had observed (he went to call on the Koenigs occasionally when there was nothing better to do) it would mean a great deal of confusion.

"Bunny, I've lost my handkerchief. Get me another, like a good child, will you?"

Bunny nodded. They would have to buy dresses, knitted hoods, and soft woolly sweaters.... The race would be over in two shakes. Then he would get the handkerchief. He could always finish what he was doing before he got up and went on an errand for his mother. It was understood between them. The smallest agate was dropping behind.

"Son———"

The folded paper lay across his father's knees.

"Did you hear what your mother said?"

"Yes, Dad."

It was a very little way to that wide green opening in the pattern which was the goal, with a chance that the smallest agate might . . .

"Then what are you waiting for?"

His father spoke quietly, but his voice and his firmness were like two unreasonable hands laid upon Bunny's shoulders. Bunny knew even while he resisted them that it was of no use. They would propel him straight up the front stairs.

"What are you waiting for?"

"Nothing."

From the doorway Bunny looked back. The library had changed altogether. In the chimney the dark red bricks had become separate and rough. There were coarse perpendicular lines which he had not noticed before. And the relation between the pattern of the rug and the toe of his mother's shoe escaped him.

The little brass clock had struck ten already, and now the grandfather's clock in the hall was getting started. There was a great to-do. The grandfather's clock stammered and cleared its throat like an old person. Once it had begun, nothing could stop it. Though the house fell down, it would go right on, heavily:

Bonng . . . bonng . . . bonng . . .

And each sound as it descended through the air was wreathed and festooned with smoke from his father's cigar.

"*Charlie Chaplin married. . . . The bride, a motion-picture actress. . . .*"

Bunny saw black clothes, a mustache and cane, feet widely turned. About the baby, he decided—it was just as well that his father had not been told.

IV

From somewhere out of sight, beyond the passageway, came a soft *tput-tput-tput.* . . . Sadness descended upon Bunny, sadness and a heavy sense of change. There was only one thing in the world that made such a sound: his steamboat. Robert was playing with his steamboat.

The back room, which was to be Robert's, was now empty except for Bunny's village. Before long, Robert would have it. Robert's clothes would hang from hooks in the closet. Robert's shoes would tumble over each other on the closet floor. *Possession's nine-tenths of the law,* Robert always said when Bunny wanted his steamboat and Robert did not care to give it up.

That was because Robert was five and a half years older than he was. If *he* said that, Robert paid no attention to him. He had to get things from Robert by bargaining, or by appealing to his mother. Only she had said, definitely, that Robert was to have this room. It was all decided, just as it was decided that Robert was going to be a lawyer when he grew up—*a lawyer,* Robert said to people who asked him what he was going to be. Always that; never a preacher like Reverend Finney, nor a doctor like Dr. Macgregor. Never an architect (Bunny was going to be that). Nothing would do but that Robert must practice law, try cases before a jury, like Grandfather Blaney. And be presented with a gold-headed cane, inscribed *To Robert Morison from the grateful citizens of Logan, Illinois.*

Nothing on earth could prevent Robert from becoming a lawyer; and in the same way nothing could prevent him from taking possession of this room. Bunny knew that, when the time came, he would have to find another place for his blackboard and his magic lantern. He would have to pick up his Belgian village piece by piece and rebuild it in some other part of the house where people would be stepping over it every little while and complaining. And his magic lantern? What would he ever do about that? There were no dark green shades anywhere but in this room. His closet had no window, but it was not big enough. And besides, where would he attach the cord?

At the other end of the passage the soft *tput-tput* came to an end and Robert began talking to himself, arrogantly. Bunny listened for a moment and then went on down the passageway. From there he could see around the corner into the bathroom. Robert was declaiming, and in order to see his face in the mirror which was over the washstand he had pulled down the toilet-cover and climbed up on it. There, balancing, he continued:

> *"And if thou sayst I am not peer*
> *To any man in Scotland here . . ."*

His sleeves were wet to the elbow, both of them. There was a tear in his stocking, acquired since breakfast. And one leg hung down, stiffly. *Robert's Affliction,* people said, when he was not there to hear them.

Years ago, when Bunny was no more than a baby, having still to be carried on a pillow—Robert was hurt. Bunny knew only what he had been told. How Robert hopped on to the back end of a buggy and got run over. And they had to take his leg off, five inches above the knee. That was why Irene went up to Chicago and came back with the beautiful soldiers, the cavalrymen, which Robert kept on top of the bookcase, out of reach.

Now Robert was rehearsing. When he was satisfied with certain gestures he bared his teeth at his reflection in the mirror and going back a little, began:

> "*And if thou sayst I am not peer*
> *To any man in Scotland here,*
> *Highland*
> > *or   land,*
> > > *low-*
>
> *Far*
> > *or*
> > > *near,*
> *Lord Angus, thou hast*
> > > *LIED!*

The effect was fearful, even from the passageway. Bunny withdrew softly and went into his mother's room to get the handkerchief. Then he took it down to her and came up again, this time by the back stairs.

V

Sunday morning was an excellent time for invading a city. It was past noon before Bunny's imagination flagged. But very suddenly the scene changed. Walls, gates, roofs, broken parapets and towers were then laid bare in simple actuality—two collapsible drinking-cups, a ruler, a block of stone, cardboard, brown paper, three pencils, and a carved wooden spool. After that it was no longer possible to pretend that his lead soldiers were shouting to one another and defending a Belgian town.

In actual weariness Bunny got up and went out to the back hall where the clothes-hamper stood, where his mother kept the ammonia-bottle and rags for cleaning. She would know some way for him to pass the interminable time between now and time for dinner. . . . He felt his way down the gloomy, boxed-in stairs.

She was in the kitchen when he found her, at the table with spoons laid out in rows and the silver polish open at her elbow. Bunny sat down without a word, and twisted his legs through the rungs of the high kitchen stool. The kitchen always seemed older than the rest of the house, although it was not. Older and more seasoned. Bunny could remember being here before he could remember anything else. The walls were dark with scrubbing, and the surfaces shone wherever there was metal or porcelain. Turnip tops flourished in bowls along the window sill.

The spoons which his mother was polishing were plain, for the most part. Not very interesting to do. But she looked through them until she found one with her name written on it—*Elizabeth*—and with roses and pineapples, and the sun going down behind the Ohio State Capitol. As soon as Bunny took up a piece of rag and began to polish his mother's name, the sadness slipped away. Now that he was in the kitchen beside her, it was impossible to care very much whether Robert got the back room or whether he didn't.

Outside, the sky was growing lighter. The rain came down unevenly, in spurts. The kitchen curtains were turning a brighter green, fading, and turning bright green again. Bunny looked up in time to see the pantry door open.

"Is there anybody home?"

It was Irene, tall and straight-shouldered in a blue coat, her flaxen braids binding her flaxen hair, like the Miller's Daughter in *Rumplestiltskin*.

"Surprise!"

He threw himself upon her.

"Nobody told me you were coming."

"Surprise, I said!"

She took hold of him by his arms, above the elbow, and began to turn. Round they went in the middle of the floor with the room tilting this way and that. Round they went.

Round his mother went, and the cookstove, and Sophie in a pink apron, and the sink . . . faster . . . faster . . . the table . . . the stove . . . the sink . . . table . . . stove . . . sink streaking longer . . . upward and longer. . . .

After they stopped whirling, the kitchen went round and round for a long while, all by itself. Always when Irene came for Sunday dinner it was that way. His mother alone was calm and unshaken. She got up from the table and went to meet Irene. They kissed haphazardly, in front of the stove.

Irene was his mother's sister, but she did not resemble his mother in the least. Irene's features were sharp and quick. His mother was dark and rather small, rather plump by comparison. Yet both of them belonged together. Bunny could see that instantly. They were like the two faces of a coin. And the things they said to each other had little meaning, often, for other people. For instance, if Irene remarked *Butter's what I'm after*—they both grew hysterical. When he inquired what was so funny about that, they couldn't possibly explain. It was a family joke, that was all—a joke so old that neither of them could remember what the point of it was.

"Have you enough to eat, Bess?"

Bunny looked toward his mother, and was relieved when she nodded. It would be a great pity if Irene went away before dinner.

"I mean *plenty*," Irene insisted. "Because there's no use in my staying if it isn't going to be worth while."

Then, without waiting for answer, she went to take off her coat.

Bunny followed discreetly at her heels. The dining-room as they passed through seemed braced and ready for excitement. Although it was only a quarter after twelve, the little brass clock in the library started to strike. Irene did that to things. Most people's rubbers came off easily, but one of hers sailed half-way across the floor. The other had to be rescued from under the hall-tree. And the moment she began pulling at her gloves there was a great burst of singing from above:

> *"O when I die*
> *Don't bury me at all,*
> *Just pickle my bones*
> *In alkyhol ..."*

Bunny felt called upon to explain.

"It's only Robert," he said. "Upstairs, playing with my steamboat."

Then by way of an afterthought, "Where's Agnes?"

"At her Grandmother Hiller's. She's there for the day."

It was not an unreasonable place for her to be, though as a rule Irene and little Agnes came together. After dinner he and Agnes played house behind the sofa. Agnes was the mother. She made beds and dusted and swept and talked to the groceryman over the telephone (he was the groceryman) and had lunch ready for her fat sofa-pillow children when they got home from school. At the end of the day the father came home (he was the father) and spanked all the sofa-pillows that hadn't minded their mother, and gave French harps to all that had.

Friday was the usual day for Agnes to go to her grandmother's. On Friday his mother and Irene went to their bridge club. After school he and Agnes walked home together—Agnes to her Grandmother Hiller's and he to his Grandmother Morison's, who lived with Aunt Clara and Uncle Wilfred Paisley in a square white house down the block. At five-thirty his mother called for him in the car. Irene was with her and they were wearing their best clothes. That was the way it usually was, and he wouldn't have thought anything about it except for the fact that Irene continued to stare moodily past the top of his head. A moment ago she was bright and cheerful. Now——

"Irene?"

Apparently she did not hear him. If he asked her what he wanted to ask her, she might not like it. She might call him a *curiosity cat*. As long as he was able, he stood and watched her pocketbook swinging back and forth on the tip of her index finger.

"Irene, why is it that Agnes is at her Grandmother Hiller's?"

"She's there to see her father."

The pocketbook stopped swinging and slid to the floor. Bunny was deeply startled. He bent over and picked it up for her, but she did not seem to want it, particularly. Agnes' father was Uncle Boyd Hiller, but he was not mentioned in the family. Or if he was, it was always by his initials—*B.H.* Never by his name. Not since the time they had to go to court to get little Agnes away from him. After that he went away and they didn't know where he was, or anything about him. Not for a long while. If he had come back now, it might mean all sorts of things. It might mean that he had come to take Agnes away. Or that Irene would have to go and live with him the way she did before. It might mean——

The singing broke out again, on the landing, directly above them.

> " ' *Tis better by far*
> *Not to spit at all*
> *Than to spit too far*
> *And hit the wall.*"

Robert appeared, steamboat in hand, singing. He had made a half-hearted attempt at combing his hair, but yellow wisps stuck out in all directions. Irene's face brightened as soon as she saw him. Robert, from the very beginning, had been her favorite. But Bunny did not mind. Irene was not the kind of person he could mind. And besides, she never thought he ought to be outdoors when he wasn't.

"Don't tell everything you know, Bunny."

Irene got up, now, and went toward the stairs. Bunny shook his head. He did, sometimes. He did tell everything he knew. But he didn't mean to. And this time he was practically certain that Robert (who didn't like to be kissed) would dodge suddenly before Irene could catch him.

VI

Irene had a way of making things memorable.

So it seemed to Bunny as his father held out his mother's chair for her and they all sat down to dinner.

Because Irene was here, it was an occasion. Like Thanksgiving or Christmas. They unfolded their napkins with a more than ordinary anticipation. What they said was of no importance; merely to pass the time until Sophie appeared with the roast chicken and the occasion was confirmed. Then there were exclamations. His mother leaned forward anxiously, lest the chicken fail to be as tender as it looked. Bunny eyed the drumsticks. One of them went to him, as a rule.

"Hopefully yours," his father said, pointing the carving fork at him. And they all laughed. Even Sophie.

Then his father considered the chicken carefully. There was a moment of tension, and the knife slid in. Bunny could not help feeling that they would remember this afterward as the best roast chicken that ever they had.

"Just give me a little, James," his mother said—for she was always served first. "And no potato."

"Well you have to eat *some*thing. You'll be sick!"

"Yes, I know. . . . At the Friday club Amelia Shepherd was telling about a woman in Peoria who——"

"There's no sense to it," his father said, gloomily. Then his disapproval passed, for lack of opposition, and he went on serving. One drumstick and a slice of the breast went to Irene. When Robert got his wing, Bunny felt that he could look no more. He turned his head quickly and focused his attention upon the Japanese pilgrims who were climbing in and out among the folds of the curtains. He heard Sophie pass behind him and go back to the other side of the table. When he opened his eyes the drumstick was there, right on his plate. And the wishbone beside it.

Happily, Bunny looked about him at the circle of faces. His mother's eyes were dark brown, like his own. Robert's were hazel. Aunt Eth lived in Rockford and she had hazel eyes also. But Irene's eyes were gray.

When she went to bed at night she let down her hair and it was golden, like the hair of the Miller's Daughter. And it came almost to her knees. A hundred times each night and a hundred times each morning she brushed it with an ivory brush. Looking at her, he was reminded of his own drooping shoulders (hers were so straight) and thrust them back. No one noticed or thought to comment on his posture, so he relaxed after a second and began to eat.

The conversation became serious. There was talk about the war, and how the rumor started that the war was over. And talk about the last election, which his father took into his own hands immediately. When Bunny grew up he was going to vote Republican because his father was a Republican, and his father before him. It was all settled that way. Arthur Cook's father was a Democrat and they had a picture of President Wilson framed over the fireplace in their library. But his father said that was all Tomfoolishness. When Hughes was running against Wilson, Arthur Cook wore a little brass mule, and Bunny wore an elephant. And there was a time when they didn't walk home from school together in the afternoon. But that was all over now.

"Smart, I grant you——"

His father poured out the last spoonful of gravy and gave the bowl to Sophie, to be refilled.

"Exceedingly smart. But he made the blunder of a lifetime when he asked in the name of the American flag that the people of this country reëlect a Democratic Congress. In the name of the flag he asked the people for party control. And when he said that he stepped down from the high office of the Presidency and became nothing more nor less than the leader of the Democratic party. If there's any greater mistake——"

Although his father looked straight at him, Bunny knew that he was not supposed to answer.

"If there's any greater mistake that a President could make, I'd like to know it!"

The statement hung on the air unanswered, burning with force, with enormous conviction, while his father helped himself to mashed potato.

"And what does it get him? Just tell me that. What does it get him? He loses control of the House and the Senate, both. He's still President, of course. They can't take that away from him. And so long as this country is at war, people should support him along patriotic lines. But there's nothing in the Constitution which gives the President right to undivided control of the legislative bodies, in wartime or any other time. And when it comes to furthering his own personal ambitions and the ambitions of a group of Southern Democrats who completely upset the machinery of national expenditure and taxation—when you come right down to it—*risk* the economic welfare of this country in the interests of ..."

Bunny twisted in his chair uncomfortably. He remembered something that he had meant to tell his mother. About Arthur Cook. When his father held forth in this way the quiet which belonged to the dining-room seemed to have escaped to other parts of the house. He thought of the upstairs bedrooms and how still they must be. His mother was eating her salad quite calmly, in spite of President Wilson. When she put her fork down, he might lean towards her and—but it was not easy to describe things. Especially things that had happened. For him, to think of things was to see them—schoolyard, bare trees, gravel and walks, furnace-rooms, the eaves along the south end of the building. Where among so many things should he begin?

Robert would not have had any trouble. *We were playing three-deep*, Robert would have said. *And Arthur Cook got sick.* That would have been the end of it, so far as Robert was concerned. He would not have felt obliged to explain how Arthur ran twice around the circle without tagging anybody. And how he stopped playing and said *I feel funny.* How he went over by the bicycle racks then, and sat down.

"At school, Muv——"

But he had spoken too loud.

"How would it be, son——"

His father let President Wilson alone for a minute and

turned his entire attention on him, so that Bunny felt naked and ashamed, as if he were under a glaring light.

"How would it be if you kept quiet until I finish what I'm saying? Little boys should be seen and not heard."

That was all. His father had not spoken unkindly. He was not sent from the table. No punishment was threatened. Nevertheless, Bunny withdrew sadly into his plate. And not even a second helping all the way round could restore his pleasure in this day.

His father commenced eating, and the conversation broke apart into several pieces. Robert began to explain about the tie-rack he was making at school.

"You take and take a piece of wood about so long——" Robert indicated how long, with his hands.

Bunny could tell at a glance that Irene was not interested in Robert's tie-rack. He was not interested in Robert's tie-rack, either. He was not interested in anything of Robert's except the soldiers which Robert would not let him play with, which were dearest to Robert of all his possessions.

"And when you get it planed down nice and even, you take a piece of sandpaper . . ."

Through the dining-room window Bunny could see Old John, who was stretched out on the back porch with his head resting on his black paws. John was very old and decrepit. In winter he got rheumatism in his legs so that he had to be carried in and out of the house. Half his days were spent in looking for bones that he had long since dug up. And often he thumped his tail fondly when there was nobody there.

Robert finished with the tie-rack eventually. And then his mother and Irene exchanged recipes.

"I stir it," his mother said, "without ever changing the spoon...."

"In cold water," Irene said, "and then I let it come to a boil, slowly...."

Once when they were in the bathroom and Irene was in her nightgown, she said, *Bunny Morison, stop looking at my legs!* Another time they went for a walk out past the edge of the town. They carried a book to read, and sandwiches in a cardboard box. At the first shady lane (it was in June) they turned off and settled themselves under a tree. Irene read to him out of the book, which was about boy heroes of Belgium. And a cow came on the other side of the fence and looked at them. When they got hungry they opened the cardboard box and ate all the sandwiches. That was over a year ago, and there was dust on the road. The air was heavy. Irene's voice sounded like swords clashing, slashing at the leaves overhead.

He tried now to get her attention, to ask her if she remembered that day when they went out beyond the edge of town. But Irene's face was shadowed by inattention. By the same vacant look that she had a little while ago in the front hall. His mother was talking about Karl: Would his father arrange to have Karl come some day next week—Monday or Tuesday—and take down the screens?

Meanwhile, Robert, unhindered, had eaten a third helping of everything. He was buttering a whole slice of bread, which he shouldn't. Not all at once. And there would be very little left for Old John.

When Sophie came to clear the plates away, Bunny noticed that everyone at the table fell into a silence which lasted, usually, while she brushed away the crumbs and until she brought the cream for coffee. Over the dessert his mother and Irene fell to discussing clothes. Something was gathered, his mother said, with a pleat in the back.

Bunny could not see what they found in such matters to interest them. He could have left the table when Robert did. Or when his father rose and went into the library to take his Sunday-afternoon nap. But there was still something that Bunny had to say to his mother. He waited until there was a break in the conversation; until Irene began thumbing the pages of *Elite*, which she had brought with her to the table.

"At school, Muv, we were playing three-deep——"

"Broad bands of sealskin—— "

Irene held up the magazine for his mother to see.

"—with a hobble skirt."

Apparently she had no idea that he had spoken. His mother heard. But she poured out a second cup of coffee and turned her mind resolutely away from him.

"It's too tight-waisted. I'm not in the market for anything that isn't cut along the lines of a circus tent."

Bunny peered across the table, hoping to see the picture of an elephant, but there wasn't any. Nothing but women's clothes: coats that were *gathered*, he supposed, bitterly, and blouses.

"Mother——"

"You could wear that, Irene."

His mother had taken the magazine and was thumbing the pages wistfully.

"But so could you!"

"Don't be silly."

"Don't *you* be." Irene was excited. The very smallest spark was enough to set her off. "You could copy it easy as anything, Bess. And with the fullness where it is . . ."

Bunny thought of the schoolyard: gravel and dirt, with hardly a shred of grass; bare trees; the bicycle racks; and Arthur Cook's sick eyes.

"Mother, listen to me!"

He spoke louder than before, and plucked at her sleeve.

By the way her hand closed over his, he knew that she had heard him. All the time. And that sooner or later she would pay attention to nobody but him. Only just now he must keep still. He must not interrupt until they had finished what they were saying.

VII

Bunny's nap was nearing its conclusion. Without making a sound, without moving, his body detached itself from the sofa. He moved freely among certain of the planets—Mars, the pink one, and Saturn with its rings. His dream, worn thin, began to give way around him. There was a moment of intense buzzing while he drifted back to earth. . . . Then, abruptly, he was awake.

Irene and his mother were having important conversation at the other end of the living-room. Bunny could tell that without ever opening his eyes. Their voices were low and even, and he could just distinguish one word from another.

"You're sure it isn't the war?" his mother said.

"Why should it be that?"

Bunny wanted to look at them, but he did not dare. Irene might notice him and stop talking. People always did. Nevertheless, there were ways of finding things out. Playing under tables and behind chairs, very quietly. Or if it was night and he was away from home, getting extremely sleepy, so that they had to put him on a couch somewhere and cover him up. After a while if he kept his eyes closed and breathed regularly, they thought he was asleep. That way he found out all sorts of things.

"Well, because"—his mother spoke more distinctly now—"because his company is ordered to France and you may not ever see him again. It could be that, Irene, and nothing more than that."

"It could be, but I don't think it is . . . I wish you'd seen him, Bess. He looks much older."

"So do we all. I found three gray hairs yesterday."

Bunny's mind stirred lightly within his shell. Around one of innumerable corners he came upon a staircase that he remembered—not the one here, not this staircase at home. He looked down, cautiously, and saw Agnes kicking and squirming in her father's arms. Agnes was frightened. She kept saying, *I want my mamma . . . I want my mamma . . .* over and over. Whose house it was Bunny did not know. The remembrance was cloudy and uncertain, like a dream remembered in the midst of breakfast: Uncle Boyd carrying Agnes in his arms and the door closing upon them. There was meaning to it, and possibility of explanation; only he never dared to ask. And then Irene walked past him, talking to herself. He spoke to her, but she didn't even know that he was there. At the head of the stairs she waited, as if there was something she had just that minute thought of. Then she fell down, one step at a time, bumping.

"*He* looks older in a different way, and sad. It's very hard to explain, exactly."

"No doubt."

"But if you'd seen him! It's as if he were thinking all the

time—even while he is making polite conversation—that he'd missed something people can't afford to miss."

"Whose fault could that be?"

Bunny had never heard his mother's voice sound quite so dry and unbelieving.

"His own, I suppose—but everything's that, in a way, for everybody."

"In a way. But I remember the last two months that you lived with him. I remember that you were like a crazy woman."

"I know I was. Though much of it was on account of Agnes. He was so jealous, you know. But when I try to remember his fits of temper, and how unreasonable he was, I think of all sorts of things that *I* started."

Through eyes that were nearly closed Bunny caught a glimpse of the living-room: walls covered with green wall paper, the floor carpeted with green to match, and a well of green shadow in the far corner of the room where Irene and his mother sat talking. He was not entirely awake, so that he saw things peculiarly. The white woodwork was un-attached to the walls. The shape of the chairs was ambiguous. At a word from him (a magic word) the sofa would curve its back differently and the chair-arms protrude bunches of carved wooden grapes. The golden bowl which was suspended upside-down from the ceiling by three chains was now the size of a buckeye cup and now as large as the wading-pool at the Chautauqua grounds. Time and again, while he squinted his eyes, the walls relaxed and be-came shapeless.

"On the boat, coming back from Demerara. I don't think I ever told you, Bess, but there was an impossible woman from Evansville, Indiana, who wore veils. And she had her son with her, a youngster about eleven years old. And every time they came on deck she'd light into him because he was sending all his post-cards to the same boy, instead of spreading them around.

"Boyd couldn't see anything funny in that, and after I explained, he still wasn't amused. Then I got furious at him—I don't know why—and wouldn't speak to him for a day and a half."

Bunny's eyelashes brushed and became momentarily entangled. Against the light from the bay window they seemed as large and long as spears. His mother got up and went over to the mantel. Then she came back and sat down again, with a box on her knee.

"Will you have some candy?"

"So soon after dinner. How can you, Bess?"

"It's my hungering neighbor."

"Oh, of course. I forgot.

"I wish I could, too.... But why should either of you get into a stew over something so completely unimportant?"

"As post-cards, or not thinking it was funny about post-cards?"

"Either."

"But it is important that people laugh at the same things. Or at least enjoy them in something like the same way."

"If you went back to him, Irene, you'd find——"

"He was there when I took Agnes, this noon. I went in, anyway. I shouldn't have, I suppose. But I thought, what's the use of going out of my way to make trouble when there's been enough already."

"More than enough."

The last time Uncle Boyd came to the house, before he

went away, Bunny saw him. Bunny was playing in the front hall with a china wolf-hound that used to be at Grandmother Blaney's before she died. And he looked out of the front window and saw Uncle Boyd coming up the walk. The doorbell rang. His father came to the door and opened it. And there he was—tall and thin, with a gray streak across his hair. And he said, *Is Irene here?* And his father said, *I haven't the least idea!* And shut the door in Uncle Boyd's face.

"Boyd was very pleasant. He asked after you, Bess, and said how much he thought of you——"

"That was nice of him, I'm sure."

"And when I got up to go, he went with me as far as the front walk. We stood by the hitching-post and I said good-by, and he said good-by and he was very glad to have seen me, and then he shook hands very formally as if I were a visiting lady from Scotland. And then he went all to pieces. . . .

"The things he said—you wouldn't believe me if I told you. Standing there on the sidewalk with the tears running down his cheeks. . . . It was a mistake. For two whole years he had known it was all a mistake. And the way he found out was that he caught himself looking for me wherever he went. In New York, in Vienna, he said. He'd notice some woman at the theater or walking in a park, and the back of her head would be like me. And he'd follow her, thinking possibly . . ."

Bunny narrowed his eyes as his mother got up, with the box of candy in her hand, and began to pace back and forth from one end of the long living-room to the other. After a few minutes she went out between the white columns on either side of the double-doorway and included the front hall in her pacing. Then she came back again and sat down.

"Speaking of the backs of women's heads—I took Robert aside the other day and made him promise if anything happened to me that he'd be sure and break my cut-glass vases. Somehow I can't bear to think of anyone else . . ."

Bunny's eyes flew open. In the nick of time he remembered that he was pretending to be asleep, closed them, and opened them again—more deliberately. The spears waved. He was in a field of green corn.

VIII

The intense part of the afternoon was over when Irene got up to go home. Bunny and his mother were alone after she left. And it was clear that his mother was despondent over something, for she stopped hemming diapers and gazed thoughtfully into the fire for a long while. Once she sighed.

At the right moment Bunny told her about Arthur Cook, and how Arthur got sick at school. Bunny heard the nurse telling his teacher, outside in the hall, that it was a clear case of flu. This time there was no doubt about his mother's interest. She sat looking at him anxiously, the whole time. And certain portions of his narrative had to be repeated.

"Bunny, why didn't you tell me? Why didn't you tell me last Friday, instead of waiting until now?"

He started to explain fully, but she had already picked up the receiver of the telephone.

"I'm going to call Arthur's mother, and find out how he is. And while I think of it, there's something you can do for me: We're out of cream. Sophie forgot to order any. And if I make spoon-cornbread for supper, we'll need butter as well. Half a pound.... *Nine-nine-two....* *Yes, that's right....* I could send Robert for it when he gets home from Scout meeting, but he may be late."

She bent down to kiss him.

"There, lover, don't look so sad."

But there was no other way that Bunny could look. It was the unexpected that happened, always. The empty gun, his Grandmother Morison said, that killed people. He would have to put on his rubbers and his coat and cap and gloves and go outdoors.

Weekdays he came straight home from school so that he could have his mother all to himself. At quarter after four Sophie wheeled in the tea-cart and there was a party: little cakes with white icing on them, a glass of milk for him and tea for his mother. Then he sat on her lap while she read to him from *Toinette's Philip* or from *The Hollow Tree and Deep Woods Book*. About Mr. Crow and the C-X pie. Or about Mr. Possum's Uncle Silas who went to visit Cousin Glenwood in the city and came home with a "man" and a lot of new clothes and a bag of shinny sticks.

When his mother read to him, her voice fell softly from above. It turned with the flames. Like the flames, it was full of shadows. While she was reading he would look up sometimes and discover that she had yawned; or she would stop and look into the fireplace absently, so that he would have to remind her to go on reading. But afterward, to make up for her inattention she would think of something especially nice for him. They would pop corn. Or she would go down to the trunk-room (She was not afraid, it seemed, of the thief drawn and quartered on either side of the cellar stairs) and come back with a book that he had never seen before.

There was one with colored pictures in it—pictures of people dancing. A sultana with a blue turban and magenta drawers. An old man in a black coat who twirled aimlessly on one toe. There were women with their legs out, their arms bent, their elbows drooping gracefully. Men with bows and arrows, with faces scarred and knives hanging from their belts. All of them his mother had seen three years ago, in Chicago. And there was one in particular (covered with hide like a goat or a pony, so that Bunny could not tell whether he was a man or an animal).

That was Nijinsky, his mother said.

But today there was no pleasant hour with her before his father came home. When he threw open the back door, the sky overhead was clear, the air thin and without warmth. Old John rose and extended his paws unsteadily. Bunny recognized it as a gesture toward following him. But having made the gesture, Old John could do no more. He collapsed feebly upon his square of carpet.

If it had been Robert, Bunny thought, sadly, if it had been Robert that called him, Old John would have come along.

Hoping to catch something off guard, he crossed the garden walk. But the sunlight was spread too evenly upon the ground and woven too firmly into the silence under the grape-arbor. Bunny did not disturb it in the least by his coming. Only the Lombardy poplars were a trifle unprepared, so that when he picked up a stick and broke it, their few remaining leaves were seized with a musical agitation.

For a second (and for a second only) Bunny wanted to climb up the kitchen roof, which started behind the flue and from there sloped down almost to the ground, over the cellar stairs. Then he turned and went directly toward the front walk. An iron picket was missing from the fence. Once upon a time he could slip through by ducking his head. Now he had to bend double and squeeze. He was growing. Size nine or nine and a half. And yet the sidewalk seemed no farther away than it had ever been. With his head down, his eyes fastened upon the cement, he started toward the store.

> *Step on a crack*
> *You'll break your mother's back*

It was his favorite incantation. He said it over and over, while he took two steps and then a long step. Two steps, a long step.

At the corner he looked up, for no reason. The elm trees had run their branches together, high overhead, shielding the street, which was empty and strewn with dead leaves. Mrs. Lolly's store was in the next block. Her porch was old and rickety and sagged in places, but it was high enough to stand up under. On the hard ground underneath Mrs. Lolly's porch three boys were kneeling, their arms outstretched, playing marbles. Johnny Dean, Ferris (who smoked cigarettes), and Mike Holtz. The afternoon became complicated—though it was clear, after the rain, and transparent to the farthest edges.

At the intersection Bunny crossed over. His knees were becoming drowsy with fear. He could go back, of course. He could go home and come again a little later. But what would his mother think? Cream, she told him, and half a pound of butter. . . . Opposite the store he crossed back again. Mike Holtz didn't see him, but he saw Mike Holtz. Saw his white face, jeering, his cap pulled down over one ear, his dirty fat knuckles. . . . If he could get as far as the steps, Bunny told himself, carefully, as he came to the steps, mounted over the very center of his fright, and closed the door safely behind him.

Mrs. Lolly was middle-aged and sagging, like her porch. She kept yellow pencils in the knot at the back of her hair. Bunny was grateful to her, as he was grateful now to all things—standing about in boxes and cases, on shelves all the way up to the ceiling. Everything was so substantial. The crates of apples and oranges, the pears in tissue-paper, the enormous cabbages. And most substantial of all—a very old woman who was worrying with her shawl.

Mrs. Lolly wrote numbers on a paper bag. When she stopped and looked at him blindly, Bunny saw that her eyes were full of arithmetic.

"Are you in a hurry?"

He shook his head. Not at all in a hurry. Not in the least. What he most wanted was for time to stand emphatically still, the way the sun and the moon did for Joshua.

The old woman, waiting, sucked at her teeth one after another until the pin came out of her shawl.

"Seven"—Mrs. Lolly went on counting—"and two to carry."

Bunny pressed his nose against the glass case. Gumdrops, licorice, caramels, candy-corn.

"In Chicago," the old woman said, as she fastened her shawl closely about her shoulders, "I hear there's people dying of influenza. And in St. Louis."

A pleasant imaginary voice said: *Help yourself, Bunny. Take as much of anything there is in the case as you want.*

Mrs. Lolly jabbed the pencil straight into her head.

"There's lots of sickness about," she said. "Come in

again." And with what was left of the same breath, "Young man?"

"Cream," Bunny told her. "And half a pound of butter."

Then, hoping by one means or another to delay matters, he went in pursuit of Mrs. Lolly's tortoise-shell cat.

The cat dived under a cracker-barrel.

"Anything else?"

Mrs. Lolly held the cream out to him, and butter from her ancient ice-box. With no reason to stay, and nothing left to ask for, Bunny and the old woman went out together. The steps were wet and so they both went slowly. When the old woman reached the sidewalk she stopped to catch her breath and went *phifft*—with her finger against her nose.

Disgust encircled Bunny's throat.

Crossing the street in the old woman's wake, he remembered the first time he had ever seen anyone do that. A farmer. Some one they drove out in the country to see about some insurance premiums. His father left the car at the farmhouse. They climbed under a fence and walked side by side through a meadow where daisies were growing. And they came to a field and the man was in the field with his horses. Bunny remembered plainly how he emptied his shoe, which had dirt in it. His father talked about the price of wheat—whether it was better to sell now or hold on to it awhile. And everywhere about them the green corn was making a sound like——

"*There* he goes!"

A voice sang out, with no warning. The voice of Fat Holtz. For that second trees stumbled and the sidewalk turned sickeningly under Bunny's feet. He ran, ran as hard as he could until legs tripped him from behind and hands sent him sprawling in the bitter dirt.

How Robert came to be there, who summoned him in this hour of need, Bunny did not know. Robert was there. That was enough. Robert pulled his tormentors off, one by one, and drove them away. Bunny sat up, then, and saw that there was a large hole in his stocking. And his knee was bleeding.

"Before all my friends," Robert said.

Matthews and Scully and Berryhill and Northway were crossing over to the other side of the street. They did not look back.

"In front of everybody," Robert said; "and you didn't even try to hit them."

Robert too was against him. Bunny looked at the broken glass and the white stain spreading along the walk, and burst into tears.

IX

The little brass clock on the mantel struck seven sharply, to make clear that this second Sunday in November, 1918 (which had begun serene and immeasurable) was very nearly gone.

From his place in the window seat Bunny observed that the rug was a river flowing between the stable and the long white bookshelves; turning at the chaise-longue where his mother sat with light slanting down about her head, and the blue cloth of her dress deepening into folds, into pockets.

When the little brass clock finished, the grandfather's clock cleared its throat, began to stammer. In the midst of this mechanical excitement Robert took a firmer hold on the lamp cord and with his free hand turned a page of *Tarzan and the Jewels of Opar. . . .*

When the grandfather's clock had finished, it was seven (officially) and Bunny exchanged glances with his mother. His father got up to put a fresh log on the fire. Then he took a pack of cards and laid them face down in rows on the library table. His father grew restless if they remained over-long at the dinner table; fidgeted; contrived ways of transferring the conversation bodily to the living-room where he could begin his shuffling and turning, his interminable dealing of cards. Bunny turned back to his mother.

"For this time of year," she said, "for November, it seems to be getting dark too soon."

She meant what she said, of course. And she meant also whatever she wanted to mean. Bunny was not surprised when his father stopped turning the cards and looked at her.

"I hadn't noticed it."

In this fashion they communicated with each other, out of knowledge and experience inaccessible to Bunny. By nods and silences. By a tired curve of his mother's mouth. By his father's measuring glance over the top of his spectacles. Bunny drew his knees under him and looked out. The room was reflected in the windowpane. He could see nothing until he pulled the curtain behind his head. Outside it was quite dark, as his mother said. Light from the Koenigs' window fell across their walk, across the corner of their cistern. If he were in the garden now, with a flashlight, he could see insects crawling through the cold grass. If he waited out there, waited long enough, he would hear blackbirds, and wild geese flying in migratory procession across the sky. . . . The curtain slipped back into place. Once more he could see nothing but reflections of the room. The night outside (and all that was in it) was shut away from him like those marvelous circus animals in wagons from which the sides had not been removed.

"I stopped in to see Tom Macgregor this afternoon," his father said.

"Seven of diamonds, sweetheart."

"I *see* it."

"Now, maybe, but you didn't."

Although she never paid any attention, his mother seemed to know by instinct when his father turned up the five of spades or the seven of diamonds that he was looking for. And she could tell clear across the room when his father began cheating.

"I did, too."

"Jack of clubs, then. . . . How was he?"

"How was who?" his father asked.

"Dr. Macgregor."

Bunny listened with quickening interest. It was Dr. Macgregor who took his tonsils out; who sewed up a long gash over Robert's eye the time he fell off his bicycle so there was scarcely the sign of a scar.

"He has a new hunting-dog."

"How many does that make?"

His mother sat up suddenly and poked through her sewing-kit until she found the package of needles.

"Three, as I recall. But one of them has worms. I couldn't get him to talk about anything else."

"Did you see it, Dad?"

His father drew all the cards together and sorted those which were lying face up from those which were face down. Bunny could not bear, sometimes, having to wait so long for an answer.

"Dad, did you *see* the dog that had worms?"

"Yes, son."

"What did it look like?"

His father shuffled the deck loudly before he spoke.

"It was an English setter."

Bunny got up from the window seat in despair; he would go out to the kitchen and pay a visit to Sophie, whose conversation did not leave off where it ought to begin.

To get to the kitchen he must go through the dining-room, which was almost dark. And then the butler's pantry, which was entirely so. It was safe and bright in the kitchen, but overhead were dark caverns that Bunny did not like to think about—the passageway leading to the bathroom, and the terrible back stairs.

"I think I'll go see what Sophie is doing."

His mother's nod reassured him. It said *Very well, my darling, but go quickly and don't look behind you.*

Under the pantry door there was a line of yellow light. And Bunny heard voices—Sophie, Karl, Sophie again. They were talking to each other in German, but they stopped when he pushed the door open. "Hello!" he said. The warm air of the kitchen enveloped him, instantly.

"And how is Bubi this evening?"

Karl was sitting very straight in the kitchen chair with his raincoat on. Tiny rivers of sweat ran down the sides of his face.

"My name isn't Booby, it's Bunny!"

"*Hein?*"

No matter how many times he corrected Karl, it was always the same. Karl never could remember. He always put his great hands together over his stomach and bobbed his head.

"That is good. And I all along was thinking—what you say it is? . . . *Bubi?*"

Sophie laughed then, and rattled the dishes in the kitchen sink—although there was no particular reason, so far as Bunny could make out, why she should do either.

Every Sunday night this same conversation took place. Karl appeared after supper, scraped his feet on the mat rain or shine, knocked once very gently, and came in. While Sophie washed and dried the dishes, Karl sat waiting with his coat on. And if Bunny came into the kitchen, Karl lit his pipe, gathered Bunny on to his lap, and told him a story.

After this unsteadying and unreasonable day when he had had so much to think about (the baby coming and Robert taking possession of the back room), after his encounter with Fat Holtz, Bunny gave himself up to the smell of leather and pipe tobacco; to the comfort of Karl's shoulder.

The story was always the same. Following the certain channel of Karl's sentences (*Already the ditch so deep was . . .*) he saw Karl's great-grandfather digging in mud and water up to his ankles. He saw trees falling, heard the great wind that blew and blew out of the ditch until at last it blew Karl's great-grandfather's pipe out—as Bunny was sure it would. And no sooner did Karl's great-grandfather's pipe go out (in the story) than the real pipe which Karl held between his teeth, a deep-bowled one, went out also. The two pipes had been going out at the same time ever since Bunny could remember. And always Karl had to stop and fill the real one before the story could go on.

First he couldn't remember what he had done with his tobacco-pouch. He looked earnestly on the kitchen table, under the chair, in all his pockets. He felt the sides of his trousers. He made Bunny get down so that he could search through his raincoat half a dozen times. After the pouch was located (in Karl's inside coat pocket, where he always kept it) Karl had to fill his pipe with great care. He had to tamp it down so that it was not too loose and so that it was not too tight. Then one match after another, before the pipe was lit properly. And just as Bunny was climbing back on Karl's lap, Sophie gave a final twist to her dishrag and hung it over the kitchen sink.

"*Aber* next time . . ." Karl said, smiling at him from the doorway.

But there never was any next time, Bunny thought, sadly, as he turned out the light and made his way with one hand along the wall until he reached the dining-room.

"I told you, Bess. . . . There isn't any place else for her to go."

His father and mother were in the library still. By the tone of his father's voice Bunny was sure they were discussing Grandmother Morison, who lived with Uncle Wilfred and Aunt Clara Paisley. He waited for a moment among the dining-room chairs until he could decide whether the conversation was worth overhearing.

"Why does she have to go any place? Why can't she stay right there while we are away? They could get some one to come in nights so that she wouldn't be alone. And that way she'd be more comfortable."

"No doubt. But they're going to close the house up, anyway."

"For five days? I never heard of anything so silly. Just because Wilfred wants to eat Thanksgiving dinner in Vandalia is no reason why they're obliged to have a man come out and turn off the water and gas."

"I know, my dear, but they will whether you think so or not."

Bunny thought of Aunt Clara's house, standing there on the other side of town. And how Grandmother Morison and he went up the narrow stairs that lay behind the guest-room door. Up to the attic which was Unknown Land, full of boxes no one ever looked into, pictures, vases, trunks, broken pieces of furniture, magazines, books, old clothes—so much of everything and so many things that he could never get more than a confused geographical impression of the whole. By the double flue were toys that had belonged to Cousin Morison when he was a little boy. These he was not allowed to touch.... By the second dormer window was another collection which belonged to Robert. Not so many, of course. Few of Robert's toys survived the treatment he gave them. No one was allowed to touch these, either.... In the far corner of the attic beside the water-tank were Bunny's own toys, all carefully put away in an egg-basket. These he could take down with him to Grandmother Morison's room, which smelled of camphor.

While she made quilting patterns out of brown tissue-paper, he played with the lovely Russian sleigh that worked on spools. With the paper-weight Lion of Lucerne. With tables and chairs for the house where the three bears lived. And there were pictures in the basket, as well as toys. Pictures of Daniel, of Ezekiel in the valley, of Joshua with his sword drawn, bidding the sun and the moon stand still.

In the dining-room, now, Bunny could not help regretting those other toys at Aunt Clara's which he was never allowed to play with. Especially the little gold piano with angels painted on it. Once, as he was going by he put out his hand. And Aunt Clara called up to him through the floor that the little piano was Cousin Morison's (who died of typhoid fever) and he was not to touch it.

"But, James, you don't seem to understand——"

"My dear, you're always telling me that I don't understand, and I do. I understand, perfectly. But Clara said . . ."

Bunny moved closer to the doorway. If he went any farther they'd stop, of course. And then he'd wish he had waited. But at his back was the dark pantry, and the door into the kitchen was wide open.

"If it were at any other time. But we'll both be gone, and you know there's no telling what she may take into her head to do. I don't really mind her straightening up the dresser drawers, even though things do turn up months afterward in the weirdest places. But when she feeds Bunny gumdrops and horehound candy until his stomach is upset ... And it isn't that I'm not fond of her or that I don't want her to come...."

Bunny's question was decided for him by a disturbance on the back stairs—so sudden that his terrified heart nearly stopped beating. With arms outstretched he threw himself bodily upon the lighted room.

X

While Bunny waited, the cymbal in his left hand and the large padded drumstick in his right, Robert beside him tapped delicately on the edge of his chair. Light shone on the polished surface of the piano, on the ivory keys. His father's hands proceeded up the keyboard in a series of chords twice repeated. Across the living-room his mother was looking at them. With a magazine open on her lap she was waiting for them to begin.

"Well, gentlemen?"

Bunny met his mother's eyes at the precise moment when his father started forth upon the opening measures of *Stars and Stripes Forever.* The flood of sound was so sudden and so immense that Bunny came near drowning in it. He caught at the regular six-eight rhythm as if it were a spar or a sustaining timber. And striking out with the cymbal in his left hand, the drumstick in his right, he tried frantically to save himself.

Ching...
Boom...
Ching...
Boom...
Boom...
Boom...
Boomdiddy-boom-boom...

Once started, the music swept along of its own momentum, carrying Bunny with it. He was helpless. So was Robert and so was his mother. The only opposition came from the room itself. What the green walls threw back, the fire caught at and sent up the chimney. What the fire could not reach, the ringed candelabrum turned nervously into light, ring upon ring.

After *Stars and Stripes Forever* came *Washington Post* and *El Capitan* and *The Fairest of the Fair.* Bunny's eyelids began to grow heavy. They were weighed down with music. He told himself anxiously that he must keep them open. He must not drop off to sleep. But in a very short while there was Karl's great-grandfather digging and digging with a pipe in his mouth ...

digging ...
and the water seeping into his ditch ...
and the air grown darker ...
and the high wind ...

———

"Now what's wrong?"

The music had stopped and Bunny saw to his amazement that he was at home, in the living-room. And his father was frowning at him.

"You can't expect to play with us, son, if you're going to fall asleep every five minutes. See if you can't do a little better."

Bunny stared self-consciously in front of him, past Robert's grave smirk.

"We'll quit in a few minutes and then you can go to bed."

His father turned back to the piano and with his left hand struck a chord, then another. They took up *The U. S. Field Artillery* where they had left off. Bunny forced his eyelids so wide apart that they ached. If his mother would only say something—look at him, even! Through the fading light he saw her hand upraised. She was almost ready to turn the page. His eyelids closed for a second and when he opened them, she was not there. She had put down her magazine and gone off, gone somewhere. The room darkened, permanently. There was nothing, he found, that he could do about it. He heard the rhythm of the piano. Cymbal chinked blindly on cymbal and drumstick beat drum. But he was wrapped comfortably around in music so deep and so firm that he could lie back upon it. He was upheld for a long time and then moved forward into a darkened air where thunder burst concentrically out of red rings . . . green rings . . . lavender rings . . .

"Oh, for the love of God!"

Wide awake now, and trembling, Bunny waited for the hands to descend.

"Go to bed, son. Go right now."

No harm had come to him, after all. His father had told him merely to go to bed. Nevertheless, it was all that Bunny could do to get up the stairs.

XI

Bunny woke late in the morning to the sound of bells: The Methodist bells at the corner of Tenth Street, the German Catholic bells, the Cumberland Presbyterian. . . . Was it Sunday all over again? Or was there something tremendously the matter?

While he lay in bed, wondering, the sky was split wide open by the whistle from the shoe-factory; by a second whistle from the waterworks. Then the fire alarm began, absorbing whistles and bells into its own terrible shriek. Until sound became general and the morning throbbed with it.

When Bunny drew his head out from under his pillow Robert was gone, his bed disturbed and empty. One last turn and Bunny got up likewise. Washed himself, dressed, and went downstairs. At the door of the library he waited, uncertain how he might be received. Robert and his mother were eating breakfast before the fire. His father was sitting in the window seat, reading the *Chicago Tribune*. His father's coffee was there neglected on the window sill beside him.

They looked so nice, sitting there. So like themselves. Was it possible, Bunny considered, that what he remembered about last night had never really happened?

"Good morning, everybody," he said, politely.

All three of them spoke at once:

"The war's over."

Confusion set in with their explaining. Bunny sat down in his place at the breakfast table and tied the napkin around his neck. In his sleep he dreamed things that were quite real afterward. Could it have been that? Could he have dreamed about *The U.S. Field Artillery* and his father beating time with his shoulders and how, still shaking, he undressed and got into bed?

After the music stopped, Robert came up. That much was true, not something he dreamed. And through the fringe of his eyelashes he had watched Robert undressing, taking down the straps of his wooden leg. Then darkness closed in around the sides of his bed and he was free to grieve. Tears came, hot and effortless. Ran down his cheeks into his pillow, until he was exhausted and lay quiet, looking at the wedge of light under the bedroom door. After a time the light grew wider. Voices rose and fell, unintelligibly. And he heard the legs of the card table crying out as they fell into place ...

PEACE AT LAST

Bunny deciphered the headlines of the morning paper, upside down.

Germany Surrenders
Signs Armistice Terms

"Is that what all the noise is about?"

"Of course. What did you think?" Robert became almost unbearably superior.

"I didn't know. I thought maybe it was a fire."

"A fire! Listen to him. He didn't even know the Armistice is signed!"

Bunny looked to his mother for enlightenment. The word Armistice was new to him, and he felt reasonably certain that Robert didn't know what it meant, any more than he did.

"It means *King's X*." His mother drew him to her. "Haven't you forgotten something?"

Hair? Teeth? Face and hands? "Oh, sure!"

And remembering suddenly the miraculous powers of *King's X*, Bunny put his hands around his mother's neck and kissed her. Whatever had taken place last night while she was out of the room was done for. It was over, like the war. His father was looking at them over the top of his paper. He was waiting for their attention.

"You might listen to this, son. You might like to remember it when you're grown: "*Great War Ended, Following Abdication of Kaiser and Signing Terms by German Envoys at Midnight. . . . Drastic Armistice Terms Make Huns Powerless to Renew War. . . . Washington, D. C., November eleventh—The military terms of the Armistice with Germany are embraced in eleven specifications, which include the evacuation of all invaded territory, the withdrawal of the German troops from the left bank of the Rhine, and the surrender of all supplies of war. The terms also provide for the abandonment by Germany of the treaties of Bucharest and Brest-Litovsk. . . . The naval terms provide for the surrender of one hundred and sixty submarines, fifty destroyers, six battle cruisers, eight light cruisers . . .*

The mention of boats . . . Bunny remembered something. Ever so long ago: August, 1914. Walking along the edge of the pool at the Chautauqua grounds, with a long stick. So that when his sailboat got out of reach . . . And his mother sitting beside the pool with Dr. Macgregor, reading a letter from the Old Country. In a sudden excess of clarity Bunny remembered everything. Even the sailboat's white reflection on the water. They were talking about the war, which had just begun. And his mother said, *Do you think it's serious?* And then the sailboat veered in the wind. . . .

"*Besides the surrender of a hundred and sixty submarines it is required that all others shall have their crews paid off, be put out of commission, and be placed under the supervision of the allied and American naval forces. . . . All allied vessels in German hands are to be surrendered and Germany is to notify neutrals that they are free to trade at once with . . .*"

Bunny exchanged sly glances with his mother several times. Then in a sudden glow of affection he leaned sideways and put his head against her arm. If *she* had been in trouble last night, *he* would have gone to her at once. He would not under any circumstances have remained downstairs with his father to play Russian Bank. If she had been the one, he repeated to himself sadly, nothing could have kept him from her. Nothing in the world.

"The most important day in history—" his mother whispered.

She did not really love him, though. She had never loved him. Not even when she told him about the Northern Lights, or about the Indian pony that she had when she was a little girl.

"—and you with your school clothes on!"

"But it's Monday."

"What difference does that make?"

"Don't I have to go to school, then?"

"No. What an idea!"

For the first time Bunny noticed that his mother was wearing her plaid golf-skirt, her favorite, which she saved for special occasions, like when they managed to get rid of the big seven-passenger Chalmers to a man who had just moved in from the country.

"There's going to be a parade. Hurry up and finish your breakfast. We're all finished except Robert, and he's beginning on lunch."

Robert's mouth was too full for whispering. He protested, therefore, with his hands.

"The trouble with you, Mom"—he swallowed hard—"is, you don't appreciate what a fine upstanding son you have. I wish you had Harold Engle around the house for about a week. You'd be hotfooting it over to Engle's so fast, and saying: 'We have to have Robert back again, Mrs. Engle. I guess we can't get along without him.' "

Robert took a hasty swipe at his mouth and got up from the table.

"*The military terms include the surrender of five thousand guns, half field and half light artillery, thirty thousand machine-guns, three thousand flame-throwers, and two thousand airplanes. The surrender of five thousand locomotives, fifty thousand wagons, ten thousand motor-lorries, the railways of Alsace-Lorraine for use which the Allies . . .*"

Bunny motioned for the sugar and cream, which were out of reach. His mother placed them in front of him and then turned back to Robert.

"Where are you going?"

"To see the parade."

"Already?"

"Sure. Why not?"

"I thought maybe you were going to wait and go with us."

"I'd like to, Mom. You know that. But . . ."

"*The immediate repatriation of all allied and American prisoners without reciprocal action by the Allies. Freedom of access to the Baltic Sea, with power to occupy German forts in the Cattegat . . .*"

"Oh, very well, then. Some other time. But come here a minute, before you go."

"What's the matter?"

Bunny discovered that above his head there was a point of dizziness—now stationary, and now circling round and round like a fly.

"If nobody's listening"—his father put down the paper at last, and spoke with injured dignity—"I don't suppose there's much use to go on reading this."

"But I am listening, James. I heard every word you said. Didn't I, Robert? We all did."

Her assurance was enough, in spite of every evidence to the contrary. His father went on reading!

"*Location of mines, poisonous wells . . .*"

Bunny sat and listened in respectful silence. His mother and Robert could whisper if they wanted to, and carry on; but he was *interested* in the war, even though it was over. He liked the flags, the speeches, and the Liberty Loan Drives. He liked the quiet and satisfying excitement of tracing battle lines across a map with red and green pins. For his purposes the war had ended much too soon. Now that he was saving peach stones, he wanted to go right on saving them; and caddying for his father and using the money to buy thrift stamps. He wanted to go right on doing everything as he had been doing it. He wanted the men in uniform to go right on marching, and the women to go right on knitting sweaters and socks and tying up packages to send to the soldiers in France. There was no telling what things would be like, without the war. They might be better or they might be ever so much worse. But they couldn't very well be the same.

The point of dizziness drew nearer. He shut his eyes so that he wouldn't have to look at it. And for some reason not altogether clear to him he was reminded of the schoolyard: gravel and dirt without any grass, bare trees, the bicycle-racks. . . . Robert and his mother had resumed their whispering.

"I want to see what makes you bulge so."

"That's handkerchiefs."

"One, two, three, four—so I begin to perceive. Your back pocket must be a place where they meet and congregate. Before you do anything, suppose you take . . ."

"Russian vessels recently taken by German naval forces are to be surrendered to the Allies . . ."

". . . in the hamper where they belong."

At the door in to the dining room Robert turned back, thoughtfully.

"Why can't Bunny do it?"

"No, Robert!"

His mother, forgetting, spoke in her ordinary voice. "Do it yourself."

And then she turned apologetically to his father: "There, James, I *am* sorry! It's just that Robert will forget, no matter how many times I tell him to— Not that way, Robert. Sophie's got one eye out for trouble this morning. Try the front stairs, and you'll get there all right. . . . You see, darling, how many times I have to———"

But his father was not even angry. The *King's X* was working, and Bunny decided, a trifle regretfully, that as long as this day lasted, nothing was going to happen to anybody. Not even to Robert, who had passed over their heads so heavily that the ceiling protested; who was going out the front door, now, with his cap in his hand.

"Never again will I read anything out loud to you! Such whispering and turning this way and that! Such *arguing!*"

"I know."

"Well, why do you do it, then?"

"Because I love you, James."

His mother turned, facing Bunny, and smiled—a curious shining smile, rather like Robert's when Robert had contrived to make him cry.

"And you needn't look so sad, Bunny, because I love you, too."

At the sound of her voice Bunny remembered for the first time how he slept last night and woke in a little while and found his arms and legs immovable. And knew that some one was bending over him. During the night his mother came to him, and bent over him where he lay sleeping, and put Araminta Culpepper in his arms.

"Son, if you're going to be ready in time for the parade," his father said, kindly, "you'd better hurry."

"I am hurrying," Bunny said. But instead of going upstairs he went to his mother and put his head in her lap, for he felt very odd inside of him. He could hear his mother saying, "*James, this child is burning up with fever!*" and he thought dreamily that it must be so. But at that moment the dizziness (which had been circling about his head) descended and became an intimate part of him. And after that, life was no longer uncertain or incomplete.

BOOK TWO

ROBERT

I

The grass under their feet was trampled and flattened down unevenly. They were hoarse from shouting. They knelt with their hands braced, with their toes balancing. Between their legs they saw the unstable sky

Nine...
Sixteen...
Thirty-seven...
and the roofs of houses.
Offside
Offside
Sixty-four...
Offside
Hundred-and-eighteen-shift
Watch it now
All right
WATCH it
All right
WATCH IT

They ran with knees high and trees spinning. The grey light of evening touched their foreheads, their thin dirt-drawn cheeks, their hands. Crying words, crying names, they fell together—impact of back and shoulder, down, on unknown thighs and the hard ground.

It's your turn to kick off
All right
It's your turn
Three . . .
Seventeen . . .
Thirty-eight . . .
McCarty's offside
Forty-seven . . .
Hang on to it
Hang on to it
Oh . . .
Do you stink, Northway

Into the clear circle of their voices Robert went, limping—McCarty's voice. Northway's voice, taut and protesting. The sky enclosed his shoulders.

Ah
Don't kick it
No
Knock a guy out doing that
What
Fooling like that
Come on
Come on, Morison, pass it
PASS it

Robert was thrown to the ground, alive and breathing.

Touchdown

Listen, after this . . .
Touchdown
It's not, either
For our side
Cryin' out loud
Touchdown
When
Time out I said
When did you
When

Robert picked himself up off the ground and adjusted the knees of his knickerbockers. Not gradually but all at once it was getting dark. He drew his sweater on over his head, weaving argument into it, and denial. They were going home now. Matthews and Scully and Northway and Berryhill (with the ball between his knees) and Engle and McCarty.

So long, McCarty
See you tomorrow
So long
Whose cap is this
So long
Somebody lost his cap
See you tomorrow I said
And don't forget
See you tomorrow

The sky hung down, dark and heavy upon the trees. Robert straddled his bicycle and with Irish between the handlebars left the field, riding now on the sidewalk and now in the street, which was old and full of unexpected hollows. The front wheel of his bicycle turned this way and that, jolting them.

"We should have had that touchdown," Irish said.

"By rights we should have had it, but what can you expect?"

"Sure," Irish said. "What can you expect."

"It would be nice," Robert said through his teeth; "it would be pretty nice if things were like this every day."

"Like what?"

"Parades."

"Oh, sure."

"And the band playing."

"Yeah."

"And whistles and delivery trucks with tin pans tied to them."

"Things wouldn't be so dead."

"Things wouldn't be nearly so dead."

Though it was Robert's bicycle, Matthews or McCarty or Berryhill would have offered to do the pedalling. They took it for granted that Robert wanted them to do the pedalling, on account of his leg. Irish never did. When it was time to go home he came and settled himself between the handle-bars.

After the third long block the car tracks ended and there was level pavement. Street-lights went on at all the intersections. And houses withdrew beyond the rim of their fierce swinging light. Robert, turning, saw the shadow of his head and shoulders lag behind, saw leaves scattering. . . .

After the one-storey house of old Miss Talmadge came the Bakers' and the McIntyres' and the Lloyds', then the driveway at the side of Irish's house, and the front walk. Irish got down.

"See you tomorrow."

"Sure, and thank your mother for lunch."

"Sure."

There was a light in the kitchen window, but the rest of Irish's house was dark and uninhabitable.

"So long," Robert said.

Irish waited for a cordon of leaves to blow past.

"So long."

Through one last street lamp Robert rode alone—the shadow of his wheels elongated, preceding him. Beyond Miss Brew's and the Mitchells' and the Koenigs' (beyond the unseen, undreamed-of darkness) was home: The porch light and the front door, the white pillars along the front of the porch, and Old John waiting in the shadows to greet him.

"How are you, huh? How's the boy?"

Old John wagged in a slow difficult circle, his head and hind quarters and the tip of his tail.

"How's the boy, huh?"

Robert slanted his bicycle against the steps and then, opening the front door, passed into the circumscribed region of the front hall. Irene saw him at once, and started toward him.

"Look out, now." Robert gave her fair warning. "You'll get in trouble!"

If he pretended to go right and went instead to the left, he could always get by his mother. But with Irene it was not so easy.

"Look out, your own self!"

He charged straight at her and was caught, before he could get away. She bent her face down, smothering him.

"All we have to do," his father said from the library, "is to keep Elizabeth out of that boy's room. Tie her down, the doctor said . . ."

Robert found suddenly that he was free.

He pulled off his cap and his outermost sweater. He would go now and stand beside his father, who did not subject him to these humiliating displays of affection. Irene knew he didn't like to be kissed. She only did it for meanness. . . . Robert was confused. The noise of the playing-field was still in his ears, ringing. When he hitched up his knickerbockers, Irene did likewise with her skirt.

"Where's Bunny?" he said, and made a face at her.

"He's sick." It was his father who answered him.

"What's the matter?"

"Spanish influenza," his mother said, coming toward them from the dining-room. Robert turned his eyes away. She was getting big around the waist, on account of the baby coming. He didn't mean to look, but sometimes he did, anyway, and it embarrassed her.

"If I'd only had sense enough," she exclaimed—not to them but to herself, apparently. "If I'd only taken Bunny out of school when the epidemic first started!"

The room seemed very bright to Robert, after being out-of-doors. He could feel the heat from the fireplace through his clothes.

"If things are going to happen," his father said, "they happen. There's no use trying to forestall them. You can't be taking the boy out of school every time somebody in town gets sick. Keep his bowels open, that's the main thing."

"Robert, your hands—" By the way that his mother spoke to him, it was plain that she had not been listening. She roused herself. "You can wash out in the kitchen, providing you don't wipe all the dirt off on the roller towel. Run along now . . . I want to slip upstairs for a minute."

Irene was in the doorway before her.

"I'll go, Bess."

"Thank you just the same, but——"

"I think you'd better let Irene go." His father spoke hurriedly and as if he were not altogether sure that he would be obeyed. Through heat and brightness Robert turned to look at his mother, who would not mind, now, whether he looked at her or not.

"Why?" she asked.

"Doctor's orders. You're to keep out of Bunny's room."

"But, James, how ridiculous!"

"That's what he said."

While his mother was still hesitating between anger and her original intention, Sophie appeared in the doorway. Sophie had a white apron on. And it seemed to Robert that she and the little brass clock on the mantel struck in unison.

"Dinner," they announced, "is ready."

II

Robert was awakened by a blow at the side of the house. With sleep still hanging to him, he raised himself tentatively on one elbow. It was daylight, and Karl's head and shoulders appeared at the window.

"*Wie geht's?*"

Karl had not spoken to any of them in German since America went into the war, and at first Robert could not answer him. He knew what the words meant, but he didn't know where he was until he saw the sewing-machine and the wire form his mother used for dressmaking. Bertha, it was called.

"Good, I guess... only I don't like sleeping in this room."

Karl shifted his ladder slightly and peered in through the screen. It was not safe, they said, for Robert to be in the same room with Bunny. And so they moved him in here, in the sewing-room, where he had never slept before. The stairs creaked long after everybody had gone to bed. And the shade snapping kept him awake.

"I have to, on Bunny's account. He's sick. Did Sophie tell you?"

Karl nodded, thoughtfully. "That is bad." And then he smiled—a fine smile that ran off into the grain of his face.

"Soon I go back!" he said, shifting the ladder.

"Back where?"

"To the old country."

"To Germany? Why are you going to do that?"

Balancing himself, Karl began to take down the screen.

"If you have not seen your father," he said, "if you have not seen your mother, if you have not seen your brothers for seven year . . ."

For Karl to be a German was one thing, it seemed to Robert. That couldn't be helped. But to want to go back there and be with a lot of other Germans was something else again. He yawned.

"How much will you take to close the window?"

With a great display of muscular effort, Karl managed to get the window down half an inch. Then he tucked the screen under his arm and withdrew out of sight. Karl was that way. And there was consequently nothing that Robert could do about it, except to kick the covers off and close the window himself. While he dressed, he entertained himself by thinking of the time Aunt Eth came for a visit from Rockford. Irene was there, too. And it was her idea that they dress Bertha up in his mother's best clothes, with a hat and a fur neckpiece, and stand her at the head of the stairs to fool his father. Then they waited, snickering, behind the bedroom doors. . . . After the stump sock was on, Robert lifted his artificial leg from the chair, fitted his stump into it, and drew the straps in place over his shoulders. Then partly standing, partly sitting down, he pulled his knicker-bockers on.

Robert's Affliction, people said, when they thought he wasn't listening.

The breakfast table was set before the fire in the library, as usual. Robert said good morning to his mother, and to Irene, who was wearing a green silk kimono with yellow flowers on it. They were talking about Bunny.

"Hundred and two," Irene said; "and he complains of pain in his eyes."

Before he had time to unfold his napkin, she turned upon him.

"Stick out your tongue, Robert. I wouldn't be at all surprised—Just as I thought: it's red. It's very red. You must be careful. Just see, Bess——"

But his mother was in no mood for joking. "Here's the cereal," she said, "and sugar and cream. Now shift for yourself."

When Robert was halfway through breakfast there was a blow against the side of the house. He was not startled this time. With his mouth full of toast, he waited until Karl's head and shoulders appeared at the library windows. Then he reflected by turns upon Karl, who was going to Germany; and upon Aunt Eth, who was not like his mother and not like Irene, but in a way rather like both of them. Only she had grey hair, and she was quieter than his mother even, and she taught school in Rockford. When she came to visit, she brought presents—candy or a ball-glove for him, and paints for Bunny.

Bunny was always either painting or making something out of blocks. That was all he wanted apparently. He didn't play baseball or marbles or anything that other kids liked to do. At recess time while they were playing games he stood off by himself, waiting for the bell to ring. And if anybody went up to him and started pestering him—instead of hitting back at them, he cried.

Bunny isn't well, his father said. *You have to be careful, Robert, how you play with him.* . . . He was careful, all right. But if he took Bunny out to the garage and they had a duel with longswords and daggers, the first crack over the knuckles would send Bunny on his way to the house, bawling. And if they played catch, it was the same thing. (Again the ladder struck, farther on. And Karl's head appeared at the third window. When he was gone Robert reached for the last piece of bacon.) He would have preferred a more satisfactory kind of brother, but since Bunny was the only brother he had, he tried his best to be decent to him. For instance, when Bunny got over the flu he was going to take down his good soldiers from the top of the bookcase and let Bunny look at them.

From this intention he was distracted by his mother, who laid her hand on his sleeve.

"While I think of it, Robert——"

He got up from the table, wiped his mouth with the back of his hand, and on second thought with his napkin. Whenever his mother just remembered something at this time on a Tuesday morning, it was the clean clothes. They came on Saturday, but she never got around to sorting them until it was time to send the soiled ones. If he stopped for Irish and got to school by eight-thirty, as he had promised Scully and Berryhill, he would have to hurry.

The clothes-basket was in the kitchen, on the other side of the stove, where he knew it would be. As he staggered through the library with it, he looked at his mother hopefully. But she was absorbed by what Irene was saying. Robert went on. He made it a practice never to listen to their conversation. It was generally about cooking or clothes, and it made him low in his mind. He set the basket down at the head of the stairs and amused himself while he was waiting by pulling horse-hairs out of the sofa. Irish would be expecting him. They had promised to be at school by eight-thirty, both of them. If he had only known that his mother was going to talk so long.... When his patience gave way, he went to the railing and called down.

"Please, will you hurry, Mom? I have to go."

His mother called back to him from the library: "All right, Robert. I'm coming." But it was several minutes before she appeared in the downstairs hall. Irene was with her and they were still talking.

"That's the trouble. I never can think of anything for lunch that we haven't already had."

By leaning dangerously far out over the banister, Robert could look down on the tops of their heads. Irene came first. His mother followed, but more slowly.

"Why this unseemly haste?" she asked when she had reached the landing.

"Promised Irish I'd come by for him."

"If that's all it is, then I'm afraid Irish will have to wait."

"Oh, for cryin' out loud!"

"I know, Robert. Sometimes I feel like that myself."

Robert put the stepladder in place beside the linen-closet.

"I'll bet."

"Are you talking back to me, by any chance?"

"No, but gosh, Mom——"

"All right, I just wanted to make sure. And try not to make any more noise than you have to. You'll disturb Bunny."

She bent over the clothes-basket, sorting underwear from pyjamas; sorting shirts, napkins, tablecloths, towels. First she handed the sheets up to him, then the pillowcases. And then she began to sing, under her breath, so that he could scarcely hear what she was singing.

> *"There's a long long*
> *trail a-*
> *winding*
> *Into the land of*
> *my dreams . . ."*

Robert choked on his own haste.

> *"Where the night-*
> *in-gale is*
> *sing-*
> *ing*
> *And*
> *the*
> *pale——"*

The song ended so abruptly that Robert drew his head out from among the sheets and pillowcases to see what was the matter.

"There's a bird in here," Irene exclaimed and went back into the bedroom again, closing the door behind her.

"Of course!" His mother turned to him, her arms filled

with winter underwear. "And no screens. I might have known that would happen. You'll have to do something, Robert."

This was more like it. . . . Robert slid down the stepladder, recklessly, having made up his mind to try the broom first. Then if that didn't work, they'd have to let him use his bee-bee gun.

When he came back upstairs, Irene and his mother were both inside the bedroom—Irene by the dresser and his mother on the edge of Bunny's bed, holding him. With feverish sick eyes, Bunny was watching the sparrow that flew round and round the room in great wide frightened swings. The windows were open as far as they would go.

"It's all on account of Karl taking down the screens," his mother said. And so far as Robert was concerned, her remark was neither helpful nor necessary. He took hold of the broom.

"You better get out of here, both of you. Because in a minute I'm going to start wielding this!"

Irene retreated at once, laughing and covering her hair with her hands as the bird brushed by her. His mother was not so easily hurried. "Lie still, lover," she said, with the bird flying from one side of the room to the other, swooping, turning, diving intently past her face. The door closed and right away Bunny was sitting up again, his eyes glittering with fever.

"Please don't hurt it, Robert!"

"Why not?"

Robert swung vigorously.

"Because I don't want you to."

"One more sparrow——"

"I don't care, I don't want you to hurt it!"

Robert swung and missed again. Nevertheless, the bird dropped and lay like a stone on the counterpane of Bunny's bed. As Robert's hand closed over it, he remembered: *All we have to do is to keep Elizabeth out of that boy's room. . . .*

"I'll tell mother on you!" Tears appeared and ran quietly down Bunny's cheeks.

Tie her down, the doctor said. . . . The sparrow escaped from Robert's fingers and with a sudden twist shot through the open window.

Tie her down . . .

And already she had managed to get in when they were all excited. Already she had been sitting on the edge of Bunny's bed.

"Oh, shut up!" Robert said, and swung his broom upon the empty air.

III

All Thursday morning Robert raked leaves—raked them toward him until there was a crisp pile at his feet, and then another and another. With no more leaves to fall, the trees stood out in bare essential form, forgotten during the summer and now remembered. By noon the yard was swept clean on both sides of the house, and he had carried the trash up from the basement. There was nothing left but to burn the dead leaves and trash together, in the alley. And he could do that whenever he liked.

As soon as lunch was over, Robert went upstairs to get his football helmet and jersey. He was almost at the front door when his mother saw him.

"Where are you going?"

"To play football." He had done all that his father told him to do. The afternoon belonged to him. It was as good as in his pocket. "The whole gang——"

"Yes, I know."

His mother went on into the living-room and adjusted one of the shades which was not on a line with the others.

"Your brother has the influenza, Robert. You may not have noticed it, but he has. And now that they've closed the schools to keep the epidemic from spreading, it stands to reason that you'll be much better off at home."

Robert nodded mechanically, and out of habit.

"I want you to stay in your own yard, do you hear? Because if you run all over town, you'll be playing with all kinds of children who probably haven't a thing the matter with them."

Robert looked at his mother unguardedly. She was smiling, but what she said didn't make a bit of sense. They had been up with Bunny for two nights—first Irene and then his father. And today was the third day, so that his fever would break, Dr. Macgregor said, or else it would go higher.

"I'm not going all over town, Mom. I'm only going to the vacant lot across from Dowlings' to play football."

"Please don't argue with me, Robert."

Don't argue with her! And already they were choosing up sides. As plainly as if he were there, Robert could hear them: Scully and Matthews and Northway and Berryhill.

"Crimenently——"

"There's no point in discussing it any further, Robert. Just do as I say."

His mother was tired. That was the whole trouble. She was tired and she didn't realize. . . . Robert went into the library and sat down. His father was there with stacks of papers around him—work that he had brought home from the office. He was vaguely aware of Robert's presence but no more, and for that Robert was grateful, because there was a lump in his throat that he couldn't seem to dispose of. He twirled his football helmet this way and that on the end of his finger, and tried not to think about things.

Maybe it was all his own fault, because he let his mother into the room where Bunny was. Maybe it was right for him to be punished. Two days had passed and she didn't look any different, but maybe it was right anyway. Only what good, he asked himself as he got up and went over to the rocking-chair—what good was all the time in the world? So long as he had to stay in his own yard like Bunny, what good was anything?

No answer occurred to him, and therefore he rocked—gently at first, then with conviction.

> *"She was goin' downgrade*
> *Makin' ninety miles an hour*
> *When the whis-sul broke out*
> *In a scream (Beep-Beep!).*
> *He was found in the wreck*
> *With his hand on the throttle*
> *All scalded to death*
> *With steam . . ."*

Rocking and singing cheerfully, Robert was well into the second verse when his father took a pencil from behind his ear and said, "If you're going to stay in the house, you'll have to be quiet, son. I can't concentrate."

"Sure."

Robert jammed the football helmet on his head and went to the kitchen, where Sophie was washing the sheets for Bunny's bed. Sophie was always disagreeable lately. She flew around with her nose in the air, bossing everybody. And if he so much as asked for a piece of bread and butter, she would threaten to tell his mother on him.

"Now what do you want?"

"Last night's paper."

"Right there under the table. And don't get the rest of them in a mess, do you hear?"

People were always saying, *Do you hear, Robert? Do you hear me?* As if there was something wrong with his ears. But there wasn't. He heard everything that he wanted to hear and a lot more besides. The newspaper was on top. He folded it carefully and tucked it under his belt.

"What do you want last night's paper for?"

"None of your beeswax," he said, and slammed the door on his way out.

Old John followed him around to the back of the house where the roof sloped down over the cellar stairs; where, by bracing his arms against two box elders which grew side by side, Robert could get up on the roof. As soon as he put his knee up, Old John whined.

"You better go somewhere else and play," Robert said, bitterly, and drew his other leg up after him.

Once he got as far as the kitchen roof, the rest was easy. Up there he was no longer at the mercy of anybody who chose to take a pencil from behind his ear, or raise or lower a window shade. He could look down on everything—on the back yard and the garage and the fence and the alley behind the fence, on Burnhams' trash pile and the row of young maples along the other side of the alley. To the right he could see the garden, the grape arbor, and the yard. To the left was the drive, and Bunny's sandpile under a big tree. Robert surveyed the whole scene carefully, before he sat down with his back against the chimney and opened the *Courier.* Page two.... There it was: "*SCHOOLS ... The school board and the health officer have posted notices on the school houses and at places about town to the effect that the schools will be closed until further notice...*" Robert felt very small prickles in the region of his spine. He read the first sentence twice, to make sure that there had not been a mistake.... His mother couldn't keep him at home indefinitely. Things as awful as that didn't happen. And so there would be time for playing football and marbles, for making shinny sticks, for taking muskrat traps down from the top of the garage and cleaning them, for hunting rabbits and squirrels. . . . But there was more in the notice than that. It meant that something was happening in town, all around him. Not an open excitement like the day the Armistice was signed, with fire engines and whistles and noise and people riding around in the hearse. But a quiet thing that he couldn't see or hear; that was downstairs in Bunny's room, and on Tenth Street where Arthur Cook lived, and more places than that. So that far down inside him, and for no reason that he could understand, Robert was pleased.... *The notice reads as follows: To the Parents ... While the epidemic has not reached Logan to any extent, and while it may seem unnecessary to many, yet after consulting with the health officer and the medical authorities your school board decided to close the schools for this week at least, in the hope that no new cases will develop and that this community will be spared any serious epidemic. The Illinois committee on public safety strongly advises this course and cautions people against gathering in large numbers for any purpose, also travelling on railroad trains except when absolutely necessary.* . . . Robert closed his eyes. It seemed once more as if he could hear shouting. *First down and ... four ... to go ...* Matthews and Berryhill shouting. And for that reason he wished (just for this afternoon) that Bunny, who was sick, anyway, had been the one to get run over and have his leg cut off above the knee.

But it was Crazy Jake that Robert heard, coming down the alley with his wagon and his old white horse. A long time ago, before Robert was born, Crazy Jake was held up by robbers who took his money from him and his watch, and hit him over the head. And because he was never able to think very well after that, he drove through alleys collecting tin cans for people. And he came at all hours. Robert had heard his mother say that lying awake sometimes in the middle of the night, she heard him.

"Hi Jake!"

That was the thing about being on the roof. Robert could see Crazy Jake, who couldn't see him. It was like being invisible. Searching steadily, Crazy Jake emptied the Morison's ashcan into his wagon. Then with his lips blowing, with his insane face pressed to the sky, he drove on.

There was still part of the roof for Robert to climb—the upper level which extended out in the shape of a ledge. To reach it he made use of the rain-spout, the window frame, and the iron hook where the screen had been fastened. When he reached the top he was out of breath and a little dizzy with his accomplishment. The distance to the ground was considerable; enough to affect the pit of his stomach. He could reach out if he wanted to. He could almost touch the branches of the box elder. But also he might fall headlong and break every bone in his body. And they would all come running out of the house to feel sorry. His mother . . . she would cry and take on about *him,* for a change. But she couldn't do anything. It would be too late. . . . Sometimes Robert fell from the roof of the garage, sometimes from the top of the flag-pole at the Chautauqua grounds. But in any case, people came running and took on over him.

At two o'clock Dr. Macgregor's car drove up before the Morisons' house. Until he could slip out of the grooves of his day-dream, Robert thought that Dr. Macgregor must be coming up the walk to see him. Then he remembered. It was Bunny who was sick, and this was the second time that Dr. Macgregor had come since morning.

Robert would have called out to him if he had dared. But he was not supposed to climb on this part of the roof, and they might hear him, inside. That was the trouble, he said to himself. Whenever they got into a state, it was always on Bunny's account. They never had doctors for him. Not since he was run over.

It would be nice if his father read in the paper about a specialist who had discovered a way to make bones grow. Not really, of course. Because there wasn't any way to make bones grow, after they were once cut off. But just supposing.... They would take him to Chicago to see the specialist. And after looking him over pretty carefully the specialist would tell his father and mother to take him home again and put him to bed in a dark room with the shades pulled down. Only, before they did that they'd better go out to Lincoln Park and see the animals.

After he had been home a week his leg would be put in a special cast, made of elastic plaster. They would have a nurse for him, of course. And nobody else could come into the room unless he asked for them. And maybe for days and days he wouldn't ask for them. Just lie there and take dark green—no, dark *purplish* medicine through a glass tube, every hour and a half.

And the nurse's name would be Miss Walker.

At the end of a week the specialist would come and measure the outside of the cast, which would have expanded maybe the fraction of an inch. His mother would cry, and they'd have to take her out of the room. Or maybe it had better be Irene. Because his mother wasn't very easily upset. And the specialist would tell them he had to lie flat, that was the main thing. Lie flat on his back and not talk to anybody but Miss Walker (who was starched but not straight up and down like the nurse that looked after him when he had his accident). Miss Walker was interested in football, so they talked about that, mostly. . . . Absorbed in these imaginary matters, Robert sat so still that the sparrows returned to fight with one another above the kitchen chimney. . . . When his stump began to hurt, they called the specialist by long-distance. He came and measured the cast and said it was all right: the stump was supposed to hurt. It was supposed to hurt now because the knee was forming. Within a month's time, he said, Robert would have a new knee.

The new medicine was red and thick like cod-liver oil, and the first spoonful made Robert sick. So that for a while they had to give it to him with orange juice. But then he learned to hold his nose and swallow it right down while Miss Walker said *That's the stuff.*

The cast began to get wider as flesh formed about the new bone. And the bone was growing, though it took time. He had to be patient and not think about it, because after a while the stump would begin to hurt again. And when it got to the foot, the specialist said it would hurt most of all.

Everything worked out just that way.

When it came time for them to remove the cast, they took him to the hospital. Dr. Macgregor was there—no, that was not right. There would be several doctors with masks on. Dr. Macgregor would give the anæsthetic and the last thing he would remember would be Dr. Macgregor telling him to take deep breaths so they could hurry up and get it over with. . . . Sections here and there needed polishing, Robert decided. The end, especially, where he woke up and felt with his hand, through the covers. But on the whole it would do. At least until there was time to go over it.

For it was late in the afternoon. The sky all around him had lost its brightness and some of its color. And the heat had gone out of the tin roof, when he put his hands against it. Like an explorer long out of touch with the world, he advanced to the edge and looked down. Irene was there in the garden, alone, with a bright blue shawl about her. He could see her yellow hair.

There were signs, he told himself. If Irene had come outside now to walk, it must mean something. Bunny's fever had broken. Or perhaps, as Dr. Macgregor said, it had gone higher. Slipping and sliding much of the way, Robert went down to find out. When he reached the box elders, Irene turned and started toward the kitchen door. She did not see him, apparently. She was going inside. He opened his mouth to call to her, but some one else did. Some one called her by her name, in a voice that Robert had not heard for years.

"Irene . . ."

The gate swung open, at the back of the garden, and Boyd Hiller came inside. He passed so close by the box elders that Robert saw grey hair at his temples, and his grey unhappy eyes.

"Irene, I've been waiting out there for hours. I couldn't go away—not without seeing you!"

Robert saw and understood everything, even the queer tightness in his side, which was jealousy. And the tears that sprang into his eyes. Irene had come out into the garden to walk with Boyd Hiller, and Boyd Hiller would ask her to go back to him. And if she did that, he wouldn't want to see her again. Not ever, Robert said to himself as he escaped between the trees and around the corner of the house. Not as long as he lived.

IV

After dinner Robert had the library all to himself. His father and mother went upstairs immediately, but he did not join them, for fear of meeting Irene. With no homework to do, he ran his fingers along the top shelf of the bookcase and drew out *The Scottish Chiefs*. It was an old edition that had belonged to his Grandfather Blaney. The paper had turned yellow around the edges, and the print was small. But it began the way Robert liked books to begin, and by the second page he was submerged, out of soundings. The lamp cord was his only means of contact with the upper air. He clung to that, firmly, and shaped the words in silence as he read.

At eight o'clock his mother came downstairs and stood in the doorway a moment, looking at him. He did not know that she was there. Nor did he know when Dr. Macgregor came for the third time since morning. Robert was crossing the bridge at Lanark and saw the rising moon. Committed to him, as the worthiest of Scots, was the iron box which the false Baliol had given to Lord Douglas, and Douglas to Monteith. And he had five long miles to go before he could reach the glen of Ellerslie.

At ten o'clock Irene came and took the book away from him. He was too dazed; he had been too long in another world to remember that he had been avoiding her.

"It's time for you to go to bed."

"Who said so?"

"Your ancient and honorable father."

Robert pulled himself up out of the chair. If it had been his mother, he could have finished the part he was reading and maybe gone on into the next chapter to see what was happening there. But his father was different.

With shapes of men and horses moving beside him, Robert made his way up the stairs to the sewing-room, undressed, and got into bed. For the first time he perceived how still the house was, how full of waiting. When he was little, he used to be afraid of the dark. He used to think that unnamable things were about to spring out at him from behind doors. Sometimes it was merely the house itself, tense and expectant, that frightened him. He was not afraid any longer. He could hear voices—Irene and Dr. Macgregor and the sound of Irene's heels striking the stair. While he was waiting for her to come up again, he fell asleep.

It was still dark outside when he awoke. And no way that he could tell how late it was, or how early. Poised between sleep and waking, he got up to go to the bathroom. What he saw then was like a picture, and remained that way in his mind long afterward. There were lights burning everywhere, in all the rooms. At the head of the stairs Irene and his mother were standing with their backs to him. Because neither of them moved, Robert could not move; until Bunny raised up in bed quite calmly and said, "What time is it?"

Dr. Macgregor appeared from the bedroom across the hall and went into Bunny's room at once. When he came out again, his face was relaxed and smiling.

"Elizabeth," he said, "your angel child is going to get well."

V

The next few days were like a party, it seemed to Robert. There were cut flowers from the greenhouse and callers every afternoon. And Sophie had to spend most of her time running back and forth with the teapot.

All his mother's friends came to see her—"Aunt" Amelia, "Aunt" Maud, "Aunt" Belle—and stayed often until the stroke of six. Robert could not remember when the library had been so full of women drinking tea and talking about necklines. Or when his mother had been more happy, more like herself.

"Having a baby," she said to him privately, "is no worse than spring house-cleaning. I doubt if we even have to take the curtains down."

He was not allowed to go out of the yard, or even to have Irish come there and play. But in one way and another (talking, straightening the magazines on the library table, poking the fire with a yardstick) she made it up to him, so that after a while he didn't really mind.

What his mother wanted, apparently, was to make things

up to everybody. She paid the paper boy six weeks in advance. And nothing would do but that old Miss Atkins, who came every Saturday with Boston brown bread and potholders (there were stacks of them in the linen closet), must stay to lunch. And the best blue china must be brought out for her.

Sophie alone was red-eyed and disagreeable. Robert and his mother agreed that it was on account of Karl. It was because Karl was going back to Germany.

"What I don't see," Robert explained, "is why she doesn't go to Germany with him."

"Perhaps she would," his mother said, "if Karl asked her to. Those things can't always be arranged. But whatever you do, don't mention such an idea to her. It might be years before I could get some one to make as decent pie-crust as Sophie does."

"No," Robert said, gloomily, "I won't."

"As for *our* going away, that's arranged now—everything but the railroad tickets. And I do believe that with the least encouragement your father would go right down and get them. You know how he likes to have everything ready beforehand. . . . The only thing I have to do is to make sure that the baby is a girl. I don't care, particularly. I *like* scissors and snails and puppy-dogs' tails. But your father has his heart set on a girl. And if it turns out to be another boy, we may have to send it back. There's no telling. . . . Sophie is going to stay with you and Bunny at night, so that you won't be alone. . . . If anything comes up, you're to call Dr. Macgregor. Only you're not to bother him unless it's something important—unless, for example, the house is on fire, or you catch Sophie upstairs trying on my hats. Do you understand? . . . You're old enough, Robert, to take on responsibility the way your father is always saying. And by that I mean it would be a good thing if you'd change your under-wear from time to time, and not leave the light burning in the basement. . . . Also I want you to look after Bunny while we're gone. See that he goes to bed early even if you have to go when he does. He's been through such a siege, you know. . . . And that he eats the things he's supposed to eat, not just meat and potatoes. . . . And you're to write once a week, and brush your teeth night and morning, and not make any more trouble for Sophie than you have to. . . . And while I think of it, how do you like the name *Jeanette—Jeanette Morison*—for a little girl?"

With his mother Robert was almost never constrained or ill at ease. It seemed easy and natural for her to be talking about whatever it was that was on her mind. She didn't stop what she was doing. Hardly ever. And that way he felt free to tell her all sorts of things—what the boys said about Hilda May Niemeyer at school that time, in the locker-room. Because he always knew that she would go right on sorting the sheets and pillowcases.

But with his father it was different. He liked his father and he liked pretty much the same things his father liked. Old clothes, baseball talk, fishing, guns, automobiles, tin-kering. When they were out in the country, his father and he turned to look at the same things. His mother liked trees and sunsets, but *they* liked horses plowing, orchards, and fine barns. They even liked the same kind of food, and put salt on everything, regardless. But if he came up be-hind his father and started to tell him something, he was always sorry afterward. It was never the way he had hoped it would be.

His father's comments embarrassed him. *I'm glad you told*

*me, son. But now the best thing is to forget that as quick as you can.
If you want to grow up to be decent and self-respecting, you haven't
time for any foul-minded talk like that....* Or, out of a clear sky
his father would say *Remember now, it doesn't make any difference what kind of trouble you run into; your father will always be
right here....* Something that Robert knew perfectly well.
And that somehow there was no need for saying.

Or else it was something that he didn't want to know.
Like the time they were alone in the library and his father
said, "I expect you've been wondering, Robert, why your
mother has to go all the way to Decatur to have the baby—
why she can't have it here at home. There's a reason, of
course. A very good one."

Robert had taken it for granted that his father would not
talk about *that....* And he had not been wondering why
they were going to Decatur, because mostly his father and
mother didn't tell him why they did things and so he had
long ago stopped wondering.

"When you were born, your mother had a pretty difficult
time of it. There were several days when it didn't look as
though she would pull through. And then Bunny came
along, and it was the same thing. But there's a doctor in Decatur, a very fine specialist, who's developed a new treatment in dealing with childbirth. I could explain it to you,
but the upshot is that Dr. Macgregor thinks we ought to
take her over there, even at considerable expense."

"I see."

When Robert stood up to go his father laid the evening
paper aside and stood up also.

"Because it's a pretty serious thing," his father said, and
put his arm rather awkwardly around Robert's shoulder.

Together they paced, slowly, and without reason, from

one end of the library to the other. After a time Robert began to feel the weight of his leg. He had only to say something about it and his father would stop, of course. But that would have meant giving in—admitting that there was something the matter with him.

So far as his mother was concerned, there wasn't anything the matter with him. If they were out fishing and had to crawl through a barbed-wire fence, his father looked back sometimes. Or called over his shoulder, *Can you make it, sport?*... But his mother went right on. She was like Irish in that respect. He never turned to her for sympathy because he wouldn't get it.

And the same way with games. His mother took it for granted that he would learn to swim and dive, so he did. And everything that other boys did. And the only time she praised him was when he won the tennis singles at the Scout camp. The Scoutmaster was surprised and said how fine it was—meaning that Robert was handicapped with only one leg. And the news got into the paper, eventually, and his mother wrote: *Very nice. Mailed your clean underwear this A.M. Are you getting enough to eat?*

Robert had the post-card, still. He kept it in a box, with his second-class Scout badge, and his arrowheads.

"Things are going to be different now," his father was saying. "You'll have to do more for yourself. With a baby in the house you can't expect people to be picking up your things after you and keeping your clothes in order."

Once they went out into the hall solemnly. And once into the living-room. And so long as neither of them spoke, Robert could imagine that he knew what was going on in his father's mind; that they understood each other. But to have his father turn on him and say, "These things happen to everybody, sooner or later. We have to expect them," was altogether shocking. Robert looked around wildly as they bore down on the walnut sofa. They turned aside, of course, at the very last minute, but it was a narrow escape.

"Your mother is a fine woman," his father said.

VI

Bunny was very pale after his illness, and he tired easily. The first time that he was allowed to come downstairs and sit on the chaise-longue was an event. Robert got out his soldiers and laid the box on Bunny's knees.

The box was so large that it was all Bunny could do to hold it. And Robert stood by, in case Bunny should want to take the soldiers out of their places. When Bunny had looked at them a short while (at the lancers with silver breastplates and silver plumes, at the cowboys, at the Cossacks on white horses with bearskin caps and rifles slung across their backs) he put the lid on. His hands shook slightly, and there was satisfaction in his tired eyes.

"They're nice," he said. "Thank you, Robert. Thank you a lot."

Robert was not to be taken in by mere politeness.

"Maybe sometime we could play with them together?" Bunny said.

"Sure."

"You take half and I take half, and then we could have a battle—how would that be?"

Robert returned the soldiers to the top of the bookcase where they belonged. He wanted to be nice to Bunny because Bunny had been sick. But on the other hand, it wouldn't do to commit himself.

"Sure," he said. "Maybe we could sometime." And went on to the living-room to practise his music lesson. Because there was an epidemic, his mother said, was no reason why he should get off practising.

For a while—for fifteen minutes, perhaps—he practised conscientiously. Then he made a series of trips out to the front hall to look at the clock. Each time that he came back he devoted considerable attention to the piano stool, which was either too high to suit him; or else too low. With half an hour still before him, he switched from *The Shepherd Boy's Prayer* to

Go tell

That was wrong——

Go tell
Aunt Rho
die her——

"Flat, Robert . . . B Flat!" his mother called from somewhere, from the butler's pantry. She was eating again. . . . That was the trouble. If they'd just leave him alone, he'd get along fine and maybe learn to play the piano so well that he could give recitals and people would have to pay money to come and hear him. Instead of that, they jumped on him—

his mother jumped on him every time he struck a wrong note, so that he was always having to go back to the beginning, hour after hour, week after week, year in (he said to himself) and year out.

When he went again to see what time it was, he fell over Irene's suitcase at the foot of the stairs. Irene was there too. She was poking long hatpins into her hat, and he tried to slip away while her back was turned. Nevertheless, she saw him in the mirror and stopped him. And this time it was not a matter of being kissed.

"Well, Robert, I'm going home today."

Robert could think of nothing in reply, so he sat down on the bottom step of the stairs. When Irene was convinced that her hat was straight, she came and sat down beside him.

"What," she said, "did you think of my caller?"

"I guess I didn't think anything."

"That's a likely story."

Irene took his hand and covered the skinned knuckles with her own. And Robert considered a place in his trousers knee—a place which was about worn through. The trouble was that he couldn't tell Irene what he thought about her caller—not really. Besides, it wouldn't make any difference. If she was going to live with Boyd Hiller again, she'd do it regardless of anything he said.

Long ago, before he was hurt and almost before he could remember, there was a wedding in the Episcopal church, with lots of people. It was after dark and they went there in a taxicab—Irene and Grandfather Blaney. And Irene was afraid that he'd drop the ring if he carried it on a pillow, so she put it in his hand and closed his fingers over it. That much he remembered. And going down the aisle past all the people—past Dr. Macgregor, who told him that he was out of step.

But there was more afterward. It was one of the family stories that he had heard over and over, until it seemed to him that he could almost remember it. When the time came for the ring, he wouldn't give it up. Boyd tried to take it from him and he said *No, it's Eenie's ring!* So loud that people heard him all over the church.

"The honest truth, Robert . . ."

Irene had to turn, they said, and take the ring away from him. But that part he didn't remember.

". . . the honest truth is that I didn't know Boyd was coming. I knew he was in town, of course. And when I took little Agnes to her Grandmother Hiller's, I saw him and talked to him for a few minutes. That was all."

Robert was not used to having grown-up people confide in him. First his father, and now Irene. . . . His lips stiffened with embarrassment.

"I had been in the house all afternoon, you know, with Bunny. And your father came up to relieve me, so I threw a shawl around my shoulders and went outside to get a breath of air. . . . When I discovered who it was, Robert, I did the same thing you did: I ran away."

A week's suspense, a week of secret misery escaped in one breath, so that Robert felt very light and unstable. It wasn't that Boyd Hiller was to blame for his accident—because he wasn't, really. He didn't know that Robert was climbing on the back end of his carriage. He didn't even know that Robert was there until Robert got his foot in the wheel. And then it was too late. . . . He thought of that every time that he saw Boyd. He couldn't help thinking of that.

But what troubled him now was something else. It was about Irene.

"It seemed to me that I couldn't talk to him," she was saying. "With Bunny so sick, and everything in such a turmoil. So I ran into the house. . . . The older you get, Robert, the less courage you have."

Robert stood up and put his hands in his pockets. He was glad of one thing anyway. He would not have to avoid Irene any longer.

"You wouldn't like to see some muskrat traps, would you?"

"Not now. The taxi will be here any minute."

Robert glanced at the clock. They had already talked away ten whole minutes of practising.

"Next time, then?"

Irene buttoned her right glove and drew the left one on—all but the thumb. "Next time," she said, and kissed him soundly on the mouth.

VII

The next morning Robert awoke into a bright cold room. There was snow on the window sill, and on the floor beneath. He looked out and saw that the walks were gone, the roofs buried under an inch of snow. And in the level morning light (which came neither from the sky nor the white earth but from somewhere between sky and earth) the maples stood out with meticulous clarity.

While Robert was trying to accustom himself to the change, his mother came in.

"I never knew it to fail," she announced as she closed the window.

"Never knew what to fail?"

"Sophie——"

Although it was a thing he had seen happen a thousand times, Robert sat up in bed and watched his mother turn on the radiator.

She's gone and had all her teeth out. Every tooth in her head. Wouldn't you know! She came to work this morning feeling so miserable and she was such a sight, that I told her to go home. We'll have to get Irene to come and stay with you, I guess. Or if worst comes to worst——"

The radiator began to kick and stomp, and only occasionally could Robert make out a word or two of what his mother was saying. When she left, he washed and dressed, slowly. For long periods at a time his mind remained stationary and entranced, while he played with the buttons on his shirt. But there were moments in between, when for reasons not altogether clear to him he thought about teeth, and how he swallowed one at the age of seven; and about his Grandmother Morison who kept hers in a glass of water at night; and about Sophie, and what she would look like without any.

Eventually the smell of bacon frying aroused him. He went downstairs by the back way, and found his mother in the kitchen.

"Was it that," he said, "that was making Sophie so disagreeable?"

"I don't know."

His mother turned the gas down under the coffee-pot.

"I didn't ask her. She was in no fit condition. If she had been, I'd have found out where she keeps the grapefruit knife. Because I've looked high and low. . . ."

After breakfast Robert grew restless. Nothing was arranged, now, or settled. There was no telling what might happen. But he had learned that in time of uncertainty it was best to keep out of the way. Therefore he wandered upstairs and down the passage that led to the bathroom, through the back hall and into the back room that was some day to be his.

No change had been made since the day he came here with his mother and they planned together what they were going to do to fix it up. His mother suggested matting for the floors, in place of rugs. And pictures of birds. Also if they could pick up an old sea-chest somewhere—a chest that opened from the top. He thought it would be a good idea if the bed were built against the wall like a seaman's bunk, high and narrow, with long drawers under it where he could keep his things. There was to be a bulletin board where he could tack up notices and post-cards that he wanted to look at. And they both agreed that the door was to have a padlock on it.

Now that everything was so upset, with the baby coming and all, he couldn't expect them to do much about his room. Not for a while, anyway. Turning to go, he noticed the arrangement of rectangular walls and buildings: the ruler, the block of stone, brown paper, pencils, wooden spools. Bunny must have built it—whatever it was. He was the only one who ever came here. But with that piece of cardboard braced against the sides of the two largest buildings and curving upward, Robert saw that he could construct a first-rate airplane hangar.

He carried out his idea immediately, and in a way that satisfied him beyond words. But he could not resist making one or two changes (more serious ones) so that the whole thing would look like a flying-field. And he became so intent on what he was doing that he was startled when he heard Bunny's voice, close behind him:

"What's that?"

"Flying-field."

Bunny regarded him with suspicion.

"What did you think it was?"

He leaned back proudly, so that Bunny could see his handiwork. It was all neatly arranged—the hangar and three sheds, the road leading up to it, the corners of the field. He saw that Bunny, too, was pleased, or at least hovering on the edge of pleasure.

"Those are searchlights," he said, fearing that Bunny would miss them.

Bunny was looking at something else—at a cylindrical box which had once contained a typewriter ribbon.

"My village . . . you've torn up my Belgian village!"

Robert sighed. All he ever wanted to do was to play with Bunny. And whatever he did, the result was always the same.

"It can be fixed, Bunny. All you have to do is build it over again."

"It can't, either. And I wasn't through with it. I was going to play with it a lot more and now you've spoiled it!" Bunny looked so queer when he lost his temper: white as a sheet and like a little old man. "You've spoiled the whole thing."

"I know, Bunny, but I didn't mean to. . . . And I built you a new flying-field, didn't I? That's a lot better than any old Belgian village."

"If you'd only play with your own things," Bunny shouted, "and keep out of here where you don't belong . . ." Blocks, kindling-wood, pencils, wooden spools scattered noisily across the floor and out into the hall where his father stood, looking at them.

"What's all this?"

"My village. Robert went and——"

"I didn't, either. I didn't spoil anything. I was just——"

"Well, never mind. . . . Be quiet, both of you. And listen to what I have to say. Irene is out of town. And I've been talking to your Aunt Clara. You and Bunny are to go there and stay while we're gone. So quit fighting, do you hear? Quit fighting and get your things together."

As suddenly as that, everything was changed for Robert. Everything was different.

He was too uneasy to remain upstairs even while his clothes were being packed. And so he wandered disconsolately from room to room, with Bunny at his heels. Bunny was looking for his yellow agate which had got lost somehow, or mislaid. And he seemed to be more perturbed about that than he was over the change of plans.

For some time Robert stood before the bookcase in the library, uncertain whether or not to take his soldiers. He didn't want to go and stay at Aunt Clara's. He didn't like it there. But on the other hand, what if the house should burn down while they were gone. . . . At the last minute he decided to take both his soldiers and *The Scottish Chiefs*, which he had finished once, and read partly a second time. When he came into the hall his mother was standing before the mirror, with her hat and coat on.

"Dr. Macgregor," she said, "is outside with his car, waiting. Come bid your fond mother farewell."

In sudden distress, Robert started toward her, but Bunny was there first, tugging at her and sobbing wildly into her neck.

"Why," she exclaimed through her veil. "Crying . . . at your age. What a thing to have happen!"

And when Bunny cried the harder, "There, angel, there, please don't take on so!"

Robert hesitated for a moment.

"Good-by, Mom," he said, though there was little chance that she might hear him. "Good-by." And made his way out to the car.

VIII

Aunt Clara was waiting for them behind the storm door.

"Well, how are my boys? And how are you, Doctor?"

Robert held his breath while she embraced him. Aunt Clara was a large woman—almost as tall as his father. And on weekdays she didn't wear any corset.

"Won't you take your coat off, Doctor? I say won't you take your coat off?"

Dr. Macgregor set their suitcases down in the front hall.

"Not today, thank you."

"When James called, I told him to bring the children right over. Because Mr. Paisley and I were going to Vandalia for Thanksgiving, but with the epidemic and so many people sick and all, we decided to stay home."

Blindfolded and set down like the suitcases in Aunt Clara's front hall, Robert would have known where he was. He would have known mostly by the smell, which was not like the smell of any house that he had ever been in. And not easy to describe, except that it was something like the smell of clothes shut up in boxes for too long a time.

The walls and the woodwork were dark, and the shades always at half-mast, except in the parlor, where they were all the way down, to keep the rug from fading.

While Robert stood with his cap and his overcoat still on, it occurred to him that he might slip out the back door and around the house to the car again, before anybody noticed what he was doing. He could stay with Dr. Macgregor until his father and mother came home, and then everything would be all right. He moved toward the dining-room, involuntarily, as Dr. Macgregor put his hand out to say good-by.

"If there is anything you want," Dr. Macgregor said; "if anything comes up——"

Robert nodded. There was nothing that he could say, especially when Aunt Clara answered for him.

"If there's any occasion to, Doctor, we'll call you. I say we'll call you."

From the tone of her voice, Robert felt sure that there would be no occasion. In the doorway, with cold air rushing in between his legs, Dr. Macgregor turned and smiled at him approvingly. "Be good boys," he said. "Both of you." And closed the door behind him.

"Well," Aunt Clara said, "I wasn't looking for you quite so soon. Half after nine, your father said. Go stand your overshoes on the register, Robert. There's snow on them and it'll stain the carpet."

Robert had intended to watch until Dr. Macgregor drove away, but he did not dare go to the window when Aunt Clara had told him to do something else. He stood bravely still, however. For they were rubbers, not overshoes. And in the second place, Aunt Clara was not his mother. He didn't have to mind her. Unless he wanted to, he didn't have to do anything she said.

"Come upstairs with me, Bunny. I'll take the spread off, and the bolster, in Grandma's room. And then you can have some place to lie down. You must be careful for a while. You've been a sick boy."

Bunny looked pleased with himself, although his face was streaked with tears. Robert saw and recognized the symptoms. And he saw that Bunny was making up to Aunt Clara—starting up the stairs in front of her as if she were the one person that he liked and depended on. Just as he did to Irene, or to Sophie, or to anybody who happened to be around and could get him what he wanted. When Bunny and Aunt Clara reached the landing, Robert went over to the register and stood on it, rubbers and all, preserving his independence by a kind of technicality while the hot air came up in waves, around his legs.

As soon as the rubbers were dry he took them off, and his overcoat and cap. And went into the darkened parlor. He was looking for a place to put his soldiers. Though it was safe (or fairly so), the parlor would not do because it was never used except for company. Then Aunt Clara raised the shades halfway and people sat about in the polished mahogany chairs, making conversation. On the piano there was a sea-shell that roared and a big starfish that came apart, once, in Robert's hands. He could still remember how he felt, holding it and trying to make the broken point stay on. Eventually, in fright, he put the starfish back the way it was, on top of the piano, and hoped that no one would notice. Aunt Clara discovered it the very next day, when she came to dust, and said would he please not touch things without asking.

All he wanted, Robert said to himself, was to see what it looked like underneath. But if he had known what was going to happen, he would have let the starfish be.

In the sitting-room over the doors were plaster heads— a negress in a red turban, and another (darker, and larger by several sizes) in a blue. Robert could never make up his mind whether he liked them or whether he didn't. And so he sat, experimentally, in various parts of the room, on the leather couch, in the big chair, holding his box of soldiers. Wherever he went, the negresses followed him with their white eyes. He asked his mother once where Aunt Clara got them, and she said in darkest Africa. But that was only his mother's way of saying things. Aunt Clara had been to New York with Uncle Wilfred, and come home by way of Niagara Falls. And she had been to Omaha, to a funeral. But she had never crossed the ocean. Robert was quite sure of that. Just as he was sure that the heads were not real heads but plaster, and the fireplace not a real fireplace, though it had a fancy metal screen that looked as if it were screwed on over a grate.

One time when Aunt Clara was away at a meeting of the Ladies Aid, he took the screws out and discovered that there was nothing behind it but the wall. Only the metal screen wouldn't go back on again. He tried all afternoon until his mother came to get him, and still he couldn't make the screws stay in. But it was all right, because his mother told Aunt Clara to have a man come out and fix it, and she'd pay for it. And on the way home she wasn't even angry with him. For years, she said, she'd been wanting to do the very same thing.

For his part, Robert liked things to be whatever they were. And he liked them to work. Having reached that conclusion, he went and stood before the bookcase, helplessly interested by all the curious objects that he saw there, and that he was never allowed to touch—the coral, the starfish, the shells, the peacock feather, the parrot eggs, the ocarina, the colored stones. When he could not bear to look at them any longer, he turned away to the dining-room and the front hall. It was nearly ten. He waited in front of the cuckoo clock until the little wooden door flew open and the wooden bird fell out, gasping the hour. Then he went on, still searching for a place to put his soldiers.

At the top of the stairs, in the narrow hall, Robert was confronted by the framed diplomas of Aunt Clara and Uncle Wilfred, and the Morison coat of arms, and a picture of Cousin Morison in his casket with all the funeral flowers. To the left were The Spare Room and Aunt Clara's and Uncle Wilfred's bedroom, which looked as if it were never slept in. To the right was Grandmother Morison's room. He stopped at the door and looked in. Grandmother Morison was in her rocking-chair by the window, and Bunny on the big mahogany bed with a blanket thrown over him. Neither one of them knew that Robert was there. The room was littered with dress-patterns, quilting-pieces, chalk, ribbon, old letters, spools, boxes and baskets and bags. *Come in if you're going to come in,* his grandmother always said. *Or stay out if you're going to stay out. . . .* He sniffed (there was a faint odor of camphor) and passed on down the hall to the room that was his whenever he stayed here.

It was Uncle Wilfred's study, as well—a narrow dark little room with a cot and a wardrobe and two chairs, a roll-top desk, a typewriter table, and a place in the middle to walk among them. The state agents of the Eureka Fire Insurance Company looked down at Robert from their oval frame, and stared him out of countenance. The wall paper was brown and like a sickly sweet taste on his tongue. But the wardrobe was exactly what he had been looking for.

He put the soldiers on top of it, back and hidden from sight. As he turned to go out of the room he was stopped by the sound of a train whistle: two *long*, two *short*, and then a mournful *very long* . . . Robert listened until he heard it again. Two *long* . . . two *short* . . . And knew all in one miserable second that his father and mother were on that train; that they had gone away and left him in this house which was not a comfortable kind of house, with people who were not the kind of people he liked; and that he would not see them again for a long time, if ever.

IX

Grandmother Morison could not remember the names of people, or where she put things. *James,* she would say to Robert—*Morison—Robert,* she would say; *have you seen my glasses?* And they would be on her forehead all the time.

When she had pulled them down, she would talk to Robert in a comfortable way about the *Lusitania,* which seemed to have got connected in her mind with the bombardment of Fort Sumter. And about his Great-uncle Martin, who owned a cotton plantation in Mississippi. And how if the Southern people had only been nice to the darkies and called them *mister* and *missus* there would never have been any war. And about St. Paul. And about Christ who was immersed in spite of what anybody said to the contrary because he went down *under* the water and he came up *out* of the water.

So long as Robert did not get up on the bed with his shoes on, or ask questions when she was involved in her crocheting, he could play with anything that he liked. And by trial and error he discovered that Grandmother Morison's room was the one place in the house where he was safe. Everywhere else a voice said *Robert* the minute he touched anything. If he grew restless (as he invariably did) and wandered into The Spare Room, perhaps, or downstairs, it was only a matter of time before he was impaled by Aunt Clara's voice saying *Robert, I thought I told you not to play with Uncle Wilfred's scrap-book. . . . That darning egg, Robert, belonged to your Great-grandmother Burnett. I don't believe I'd play catch with it, if I were you. Not right now, anyway. . . . Robert, do you really think that's a nice kind of a song for you to be singing. . . .* Until he was afraid to do or say anything, so he sat in the front hall folding and unfolding his hands. Or stood with his nose to the front window, watching the children pass—running, sliding, pushing each other on the icy walks.

He knew all of them by name. The boys who dragged sleds after them, and the little girls who made angels in the snow. He knew what marbles some of the older boys had in their pockets. But if they looked up and saw him, there was no flash of recognition. Nothing but wonder, as though they were looking at a Chinaman. He was cut off from them, estranged. Their mothers had not gone to Decatur to have a baby.

When there was nothing out-of-doors to interest him, Robert would turn and wait for the cuckoo clock to strike. The wooden door flew open, and the noisy little bird fell out, and that restored his interest in living. Also it reminded him of how he let his mother into the room where Bunny was—a thing he would rather have forgotten. When that escaped from his mind, he was still aware vaguely that there was something he *had* been worrying about.

One day became for him hopelessly like another. Even

Thanksgiving, because Aunt Clara had roast chicken instead of turkey, which was sixty cents a pound. But on the Saturday after Thanksgiving he made a discovery; something that he had overlooked. Under the table in the living-room was an unabridged dictionary, and on top of it seven or eight smaller books arranged according to size. He took them all off at once, in such a way that he could put them back again the instant he heard Aunt Clara coming.

Finding the wrong kind of words in the dictionary was not a crime. They couldn't put him in jail for it. But it was a thing he would not want to be caught doing, especially by Aunt Clara. It was like telling lies or listening to people who didn't know he was there.

The best way was to pick a letter (like *C*), close his eyes, and turn to whatever page he came to: *chilblain . . . child . . . childbearing . . . childbed . . . childbirth . . .* He had gone past what he was looking for. "With child," people said. A woman was with *child* (*chīld*) *n.; pl.* children (*chĭl'drĕn*) . . . *1. An unborn or recently born human being; fetus; infant; baby . . . A young person of either sex, esp. one between infancy and youth; hence, one who exhibits the characteristics of a very young person, as innocence. . . .*

Robert flushed. He looked around at the empty chairs in the sitting-room and was on the verge of closing the dictionary. Then he thought better of it.

obedience, trustfulness, limited understanding, etc. . . . "When I was a child, I spake as a child, I understood as a child. . . ." His skin felt warm, under his clothing. He had gone too far again: fetus was the word . . . *fetter . . . fettle, fettle . . . fettling . . . fetus, foetus (fē'tŭs), n. a bringing forth, brood, offspring, young ones; cf. fetus fruitful, fructified, that which is or was filled with young . . . the young or embryo of an animal in the womb. . . .* Bunny came up behind him, so quietly that Robert did not even know he was in the room. Bunny waited a moment, and then made a slight noise. Robert slammed the book together, in panic.

"If she catches you," Bunny said, "if she finds out you've been using her dictionary, you'll get hail columbia!"

"She won't find out."

"What'll you do if she does?"

"Nothing."

"Why are you so red in the face, then?"

"I'm not."

"You are, too."

"I'm not, either. For cryin' out loud, Bunny, go play somewhere!"

"I will," Bunny said, hopefully, "if you'll let me have your good soldiers?"

"Nothing doing."

"We could play with them together, maybe?"

The page was creased where Robert had been reading. He put it back carefully. It might be some time before Aunt Clara used the dictionary, and then she might not be looking for a word that began with *C* . . . *The young,* he read, *or embryo of an animal in the womb.* . . .

"We could have a battle?"

"Nothing doing, I said."

Without show of anger or resentment, Bunny went out of the room, leaving Robert free to thumb through the *W's* . . . *wolves* . . . *wolvish* . . . *woman* . . . *woman's rights* . . . *womb* . . . *The belly* . . . *The abdomen* . . . "*Transgressors from the womb*"—*Cowper* . . . *Any cavity like a womb in containing and enveloping.* . . . Robert read and reread, skipping the brackets and the abbreviations but with never a glimpse of the meaning. It was like being at a party, he thought, where they put a blindfold over his eyes and let him try to pin a tail on a donkey. The meaning was there, but he could not get at it. It was inside the words.

What Robert wanted, suddenly, was to be outdoors in a vacant field, running. He wanted to be running hard, and with a football against his ribs, to be tackled and thrown on something hard like the ground. With a sigh, he closed the dictionary, and put the other books on top of it. Then he went to the front door to see if the mail had come. It had, and there was a letter for Aunt Clara, in his father's handwriting. Robert took it to her, and waited, with his heart pounding inside his shirt.

"It's from your father," she said, as she wiped her hands on the roller towel in the kitchen. "I say it's a letter from your father." She opened the letter and read it from beginning to end, slowly. When she had finished, she put it back in the envelope and the envelope in the pocket of her kitchen apron.

"Has the baby come?" Robert asked, for he could not hold himself in any longer.

"No."

"Does he say how my mother is?"

"Your mother is fine—getting along as well as can be expected, he says."

Robert looked at her.

"Is that all he says?"

"Yes, that's all...."

But it wasn't, Robert assured himself on his way upstairs. He could tell by her eyes. There was something in that letter which Aunt Clara hadn't told him. He might go to the phone and call Dr. Macgregor, perhaps, and find out how things were. But his mother said not to bother him unless it was something important and this might not be.

But then again, Robert said to himself as he reached the head of the stairs, it might. He turned down the hall and saw at once that Bunny was trying to get at his soldiers. Bunny had pulled Uncle Wilfred's swivel-chair across the study and was teetering on it, in front of the wardrobe.

"Hey!"

Bunny turned a frightened face upon him and lost his balance. The soldiers fell with him, all the way to the floor.

"I didn't go to . . . really I didn't!"

Robert brushed past him without a word. There were his Cossacks with arms broken off, and heads, and rifles, and the legs of their white horses. His mouth twisted in pity. There were his lancers.

"Damn you," he said. "Damn you, Bunny . . . *Damn* you!"

X

With glue and matches, wire, toothpicks, and pieces of thread Robert worked over his broken soldiers all Sunday morning. Fortunately the legs of certain horses were all in one piece. He could make those legs stay on. And if the horses wouldn't stand up afterward, he could always pretend that they were lame. Arms could be fastened on with wire, and heads with matches. So that when anyone stood off at a distance from them, he could hardly tell that the soldiers were mended. The trouble was that Robert didn't play with them standing off at a distance.

Bunny wanted to help, but Aunt Clara said no, Robert didn't deserve any help after speaking to his brother like that—which was all right with Robert. When Bunny got big enough so that they were both grown up and the same size, he was going to take Bunny out in the back yard and clean up on him. That might not put any soldiers back together again, he told himself (and Bunny), but it would certainly make him feel a lot better. Because every so often, with the soldiers spread around him on the sitting-room

floor—an arm here and part of a sword or a helmet there—
he would get crazy mad and decide it was too long a time
to wait until Bunny grew up, and something could be done
right then and there. Uncle Wilfred was sitting in the big
chair, with the Sunday paper. And so nothing was.

At five minutes to one, Aunt Clara called Robert and
Bunny to come wash their hands for dinner. Bunny got to
the kitchen sink first and took so long that it was time to sit
down before Robert had his turn at the soap. He did not
feel obliged, therefore, to wash with any great thorough-
ness or be too particular about not leaving any dirt on the
roller towel. Besides, he said to himself as he sat down and
unfolded his napkin, he was hungry.

At home it wasn't considered cheating if he started in on
his salad before everyone else had been served. Not especially. There was no reason why it should be here. But no
sooner did he commence than Aunt Clara spoke to him in
a hushed voice.

"Robert, you've forgotten something."

He glanced up in surprise and saw that they were all
looking at him—Aunt Clara, Uncle Wilfred, Grandmother
Morison, and Bunny. With a sigh he put down his salad fork
and bowed his head, while Uncle Wilfred in a disapproving
voice said, "Bless us, O Lord, and these thy gifts. . . ."

Even after the blessing had been asked and they were
free to receive it, Uncle Wilfred was not restored to a good
humor. So far as Robert could make out, *he* was not responsible. It was the health officer, who had requested that for
the duration of the epidemic the First Baptist Church (together with all the other churches) close its doors. To
Uncle Wilfred's mind, there was no need for such action.

"It's one thing," he said, passing over the wing which was

Robert's favorite piece of chicken and giving him the drumstick, which he never ate if he could help it; "it is one thing to close the bowling-alley and the pool-halls. But to close the church of Jesus Christ is something else again. Anybody would think that church gatherings are un-healthy—that they're particularly conducive to the spread of disease."

"Of course it's true," Aunt Clara said, "there's lots of sickness about. Fourteen from the two banks, the paper said. And four or five of those employed at the Spitley house."

"And two from the post-office," Grandmother Morison offered. Without exactly rejecting Grandmother Morison's two from the post-office, Uncle Wilfred helped himself to beans and mashed potatoes.

"Church," he said, "is of so little importance that they can afford to suspend it at the slightest pretext.... There's no reason that I can see why people who come together for an hour on Sunday should be any more exposed to disease than they are all day long in stores and offices."

"Or even as much," Aunt Clara said, firmly.

Robert looked from one to the other. He was not hungry now. While they were talking, all desire for food left him.

"It's cold in here," he said, not expecting that Aunt Clara would get up and go look at the thermometer.

"I declare ... seventy-six. Don't you feel well, Robert?"

He was all right. Perfectly. There was no reason why they should all be staring at him that way.

"Your eyes look kind of bloodshot."

Robert pushed his chair back from the table. "No," he said, "I just thought it was cold in here." And before he could get upstairs to the bathroom, he was vomiting.

Aunt Clara undressed him, as much as he would let her; and pulled the covers back so that he could get into bed. In a little while Dr. Macgregor came and took his temperature and asked him questions—all from too great a distance to be of any help. Robert was glad that Dr. Macgregor had come, and sorry when he went away. But there was nothing that he could do about it. He was cut loose. He was adrift utterly in his own sickness.

For three days and three nights it was like that.

Aunt Clara appeared every two hours—now fully dressed, and now in a long white nightgown with her hair in braids down her back. Sometimes her coming was so slight an interruption that he could not be sure afterwards whether she had been there at all. Again she stood beside his bed for an indefinite time, with two white tablets in one hand and a glass of water in the other.

On the morning of the fourth day Robert awoke from a sound sleep and knew that he was better. He knew also that there was something that he had to find out, as soon as he could remember what it was. Aunt Clara appeared with his breakfast tray.

"Good-morning," she said. "How do you feel? I say how are you feeling, Robert?"

"Better."

His voice sounded weak and like the voice of somebody else.

"I think I'll get up, Aunt Clara."

"You'll do no such thing. . . . Stay in bed like the doctor told you, and take your medicine, or you can't tell what may happen. You've been a sick boy, Robert. A mighty sick . . ."

The letter. . . . Quite suddenly it came to him. Aunt Clara got a letter and she wouldn't tell him what was in it. He was going to call Dr. Macgregor and find out how things were. And when Dr. Macgregor came, he was too sick to remember it.

"Aunt Clara, can you tell me how my mother is?"

"She's getting along fine, the doctor says. As well as can be expected."

Robert was not at all satisfied. As soon as she went out of the room, he turned his back to the wall, so that he would not have to look at the insurance agents, and slept. At noon Aunt Clara awakened him to give him his medicine. He asked her the same question and got a similar answer. He closed his eyes and slept and woke up again and slept again until he had disposed of the greater part of a winter afternoon. The street lamp shone in squares upon the ceiling. Turning then, Robert saw (distantly, as through the wrong end of opera glasses) things that had taken place a month before. The last Sunday in October they wedged themselves into the car, among fishing-poles, baskets of food, skillets, automobile robes, water-bottles, and worms. Then drove out into the country until they came to a special gate. After that they had to crawl through a barbed-wire fence and lug all they had brought with them to a clearing on the banks of a creek.

With the automobile robes spread out on the ground and the food put away, his father went far down the creek to cast for pickerel and bass. His mother sat on a high bank where all the sunfish in the creek would come, sooner or later, to nibble the bait off her hook. Bunny sat near her among the roots of an old tree. And Robert went up the creek and over a bridge (between the bridge and a sycamore tree) where he could cast without getting his line caught in the overhanging branches.

His mother smiled at him foolishly from the opposite bank. And it seemed to him that she was smiling at the sky also, and at the creek, and at the yellow leaves which came down, sometimes by the dozen, and sailed in under the bank and out again.

XI

When Robert awoke it was quite dark outside, and what Aunt Clara was saying downstairs came up to him, distinctly, through the register.

"Yes. . . . Yes, Amanda. . . ."

Her voice was pitched for the telephone.

"I'm pretty well. How are you? . . . I say I'm pretty well. . . . Yes . . . he's better, I think . . . I say Robert's better. Been asleep off and on most of the day. . . . Yes . . . in Decatur. . . . Yes . . . in spite of every precaution . . . both of them . . . James, too. . . ."

Robert sank back on the pillow. It was his mother and father that they were talking about. Something had happened to his mother and father while he was sick. Or before, maybe. And Aunt Clara wouldn't tell him. When she came up with his dinner he would say *How is my mother?* And Aunt Clara would put the tray down on Uncle Wilfred's desk before she answered him. *I told you,* she would say. *Your mother is getting along as well as can be expected.* . . . But that was not the way that things worked out. Before it was time for his tray, Robert heard the front-door bell ring, and Irene's voice in the downstairs hall. He sat up in bed feeling very dizzy and not altogether sure that what he heard was not imagined.

"I don't know, Irene . . ."

Aunt Clara was arguing with her.

"I say I don't know whether Robert ought to see anybody or not. He's still running a temperature and the doctor's orders are that——"

Robert could not bear it another second.

"Irene," he called, "I'm up here!"

He heard the sound of heels upon the stair, and knew beyond all doubt that there was one person in the world who was not afraid of Aunt Clara.

Irene switched the light on. She was very beautiful as she stood in the doorway. Her eyes were shining and she was all in black, with a black fur around her neck. She came and sat down on the bed, beside him, and Robert could smell lavender. That was a joke. Everything, suddenly, had become a joke. His hands (which she was holding) and the dun-colored wall paper, the insurance agents, and most of all Robert himself—for being foolish enough to get sick at such a place as Aunt Clara's.

"I've been to Chicago," Irene said, as if that too were foolish.

So much had happened since she sat on the stairs with him. He did not ask why she had gone to Chicago. He did not care. When he was little and did something that he shouldn't—like turning the hose on Aunt Eth, who was starting out to the Friday Bridge Club—he set out for Irene's as fast as he could go. If he got there, he was safe. Irene would not let anybody come near him. Her eyes blazed and she put him behind her and said, *James Morison, don't you touch a hair of this child's head!"*

Robert looked at Irene carefully, trying to memorize her face and the buckle on her hat so that he would have something when she was gone. In her handkerchief there was a sponge soaked in powder, like the one his mother carried. He listened with only a part of his mind to the story that she was telling—how she got lost on the street in Chicago.

". . . When I was sure that I didn't have the vaguest idea where I was, I went up to a policeman and said *Can you please tell me how to get back to the Palmer House?* And he said *Lady, follow your nose."*

Robert smiled and spoke her name slowly.

"Irene . . ."

"What is it?"

"There's a girl who called here a little while ago. Her name is Amanda Matthews."

"Yes, Robert."

"They talked about my mother. . . . When I ask Aunt Clara how she is, Aunt Clara always says *getting along as well as can be expected."*

He could not frame the question that was troubling him. But Irene seemed to know anyway. She nodded to him just as if he had spoken it aloud.

"Turn over," she said. Then she pulled the covers down and rubbed his back the way she used to do when he was little—rubbed it until he felt drowsy and quiet, far inside of him.

"Your mother and father both have influenza and they're very sick."

When he turned around to look at her, she smiled. This too was going to be a joke.

"Your mother has double pneumonia. The baby was born yesterday . . . is still alive. I talked to the doctor this noon. He said that your mother was slightly improved. . . . She has an even chance, he said."

Robert turned his back to the wall and closed his eyes. He had found out now what it was that he wanted to know.

XII

After Irene had gone, Robert sought in his mind and in his fever for a way to explain the situation. He did not want to use certain words that frightened him. *Double pneumonia,* Irene had said. And both his father and his mother were in the hospital.

And there was "Aunt" Amelia's husband, for instance. Mr. Shepherd had pneumonia (the plain kind) winter before last and there was something called *the crisis.* When that was over, he got well. But people didn't always.

Miss Harris at school didn't get well. She had "*T.B.*" and that was why she was so pale. She taught geography and all the kids used to bring her apples and oranges. And lilacs when they were in bloom. She asked them to wait until the lilac blossoms had opened before they picked them, because lilacs don't open in water, she said. But sometimes they couldn't wait. And for her birthday the whole class gave her sweet peas from the greenhouse.

When she had to stop teaching, Robert and Irish rode out to see her one afternoon on his bicycle. She was in a downstairs room, in bed, and she had changed so much during that short time that they hardly knew her. She coughed when she tried to talk to them. And there was a clock in the room that ticked loudly, and they were not allowed to stay but a minute or two.

That was several years ago. Before that Robert could remember about his Grandfather Blaney. Out in the country at a place called Gracelands they kept a ferret to drive the rats away. The ferret bit Grandfather Blaney in the ear while he was sleeping. Then he came home and was sick a long time, so that they had to have the Christmas tree upstairs in his room. When the door was opened, Bunny and Agnes rushed in together—Agnes crying *See my rocking-horse,* and Bunny *Oh, see my doll!*

For months Grandfather Blaney was sick in that room at the head of the stairs. Then he died and the door was kept tightly closed. Robert opened it once when there was nobody around, and went inside. They had taken everything out of the room except the furniture. There weren't even any clothes in the clothes-closet.

When he went home, he talked to his mother about it. She told him how they thought Grandfather Blaney was dead, and how he opened his eyes and looked at them and said, *Heaven is a providing-place. . . .* That was very much like something Mr. Stark read in Sunday school: *In my Father's house are many mansions.* The same thing, practically. If people were good, Mr. Stark said, and didn't break the Ten Commandments—why, when they died they went to Heaven. Cats and dogs, too. Only that wasn't right. Robert knew that for certain because Irish's cat had kittens that had to be killed. And he and Irish buried one of them in a Mason jar with a little water in it. . . .

There were some things it was better not to think about. Without thinking at all, therefore, Robert lay quietly while moment after moment rose over him and set. Some one came upstairs. He heard the toilet being flushed and the sound of water running in the bathroom. Then there was no sound at all, until Uncle Wilfred brought his dinner up to him.

He would have liked to talk about his mother, but he didn't feel that he knew Uncle Wilfred well enough. Uncle Wilfred was kind and all that. He didn't force medicine down Robert's throat before he was half awake. And when he turned the light on, he always put a piece of paper around it. But on the other hand, Uncle Wilfred wasn't like other men. He didn't smoke or drink whisky or tell stories about how there were two Irishmen named Pat and Mike. He didn't have his hair cut often enough and he didn't believe in dancing. He wore shoes that turned up at the toe and he went to church three times on Sunday and there wasn't much of anything that Robert could talk to him about.

Each of them remained in a separate silence while Robert ate. But the moment Uncle Wilfred went out of the room, Robert was sorry that he had let Uncle Wilfred go. For he remembered, as soon as the light was turned out, that if anything happened to his mother, it would be *his* fault. He was frightened, then—more so than he had ever been. A terrible kind of fright, as if he were going to cry and be sick at his stomach, both at once. He doubled up his fists and buried his face in the hot pillow. The darkness was suffocating, but he stayed that way until he fell asleep, into a dream canopied with light.

He had come home.

He was in the little sewing-room at the head of the stairs.

It was night.

Waiting to go to sleep, he heard the stairs creaking.

And voices on the stairs.

The voices of his aunts, saying *Robert can't . . . Robert can't say . . . can't say fevver . . .* Aunt Clara, Aunt Eth who lived in Rockford, Irene. Their voices elongated in the dark and yet recognizable, saying the same thing one after another.

It made him uneasy. He turned, clutching the hem of his blanket.

Feather . . . Feather . . .

He could say it now without any trouble. Light as a . . . but not when he was little.

Feather . . .

The word snapped, conclusively.

Feather . . .

It scraped against the dark side of the house and there was laughter on the stairs.

Feather . . .

The night wind bound him, dark, divided, on his hollow bed. Unwillingly, having premonitions of anguish, he settled farther into sleep.

In his dream he heard ringing, hoofs clopping, clopping on hard pavement. . . . He saw Dreyfus with his brown flanks shining. He heard Dreyfus with his harness jigging. . . . With faces white and intent Boyd and Irene drove past him in a high black carriage. He ran after them, crying *Irene! Irene!* but they did not hear him. And so he tried to climb on the back end of the carriage, crying

Irene!

(wildly)

As the wheels, turning

Do you hear me, Irene?

dragged him . . .

Torn bodily, torn by the roots out of his dream, he sat up in the dark. Some one was shaking him.

Robert darling, wake up!

It was his mother.

I am awake.

You're not.

I am, too.

Then tell me what's the matter?

Sighing, he lay back upon the pillow. The bedsprings creaked under his dead weight. He was very tired.

I don't know . . . I was having a bad dream.

I heard you, clear in my room.

She bent over him in the dark and brushed the hair back from his forehead.

It must have been a very bad dream.

Yes, it was.

Sleep was still under him, like a pit.

He could look down. . . .

If his mother would only stay with him, he would not drop into it, immediately, and dream that same dream. But he could not ask her to do that. He was too old. Much too old.

It's this room, Robert.

She seemed to have guessed, anyway.

Without his having to tell her, she went to the window and adjusted the shade so that it wouldn't snap.

You're not used to sleeping in this room.

She came back then, and sat down beside him on the edge of the bed.

His head cleared.

His lungs were no longer expanding and contracting with excitement.

When he was quite calm inside, he started down. . . . He was not afraid now. His mother was there, and she was not going away just yet. There was no need to hurry.

Once he looked back, trying to say good-night to her, but no words came.

He had gone too far.

There was too great a distance between them.

At the very bottom, he turned and saw that she was still sitting on the edge of the bed where he had left her.

After that he did not mind.

Not even when she got up and crossed the hall and went into the room where Bunny lay sleeping.

XIII

Robert was not supposed to get up. Tomorrow, Dr. Macgregor said, if he didn't have any fever. But it was not hard. So long as Robert braced his arms against the side of the bed, he felt all right. It was only when he stood. Or when he bent over to pull on his stocking. He had to rest a little. And again before he could finish tying his shoe. Then he stood, one-legged and shivering, while he measured the distance across the room to the wardrobe where Aunt Clara had hung his suit. The floor tilted slightly, not any more than he had expected and not enough to make him fall. He drew on his underwear and his shirt. While he was adjusting the straps of his leg, a sparrow came to peck at a grain of paint on the window sill and Robert waved his arms, weakly, to frighten it away.

Before he had finished dressing, the telephone rang and Aunt Clara's voice came up through the register. Robert drew his belt on and buckled it, listening.

"Hello. . . . Hello, James, I can't hear you . . . I say I can't hear you very well. Can you hear me? . . . Yes. . . ."

At the thought of his father Robert had to sit down and with both hands cling to the edge of the chair.

"You don't mean it, James. . . ." And then a long silence and, "No, but I will . . . if you want me to."

Straining, Robert heard the click of the receiver. The stairs creaked softly.

"Bunny . . . *Oh*, Bunny. . . ."

Aunt Clara was already at the head of the stairs when Robert pulled his door open. She was neither surprised to see him nor angry.

"Come in here, Robert," she said. "I have something to tell you."

He followed her into Grandmother Morison's room. Bunny was there alone. And he was in his pyjamas. Aunt Clara sat down in the rocking-chair and gathered Bunny to her lap.

"It's about your mother," she said.

Her voice sounded hoarse, as if she had a cold. She began to rock back and forth, back and forth, until her eyes covered over with tears. Robert turned then and went out of the room.

He did not have to be told what had happened. He knew already. His mother was dead. During the night while he was sleeping, she got worse. Then she did not have an even chance, like the doctor said. And she died.

When Robert had found his way to the head of the stairs, he started down, one step at a time.

His head roared grandly like the shell in the parlor. He reached out for the weights, the cone-shaped weights of the cuckoo clock, and clung to them, swaying, until space formed and the earth was solid under his feet.

BOOK THREE

UPON A
COMPASS-POINT

I

If James Morison had come upon himself on the street, he would have thought *That poor fellow is done for.* . . . But he walked past the mirror in the front hall without seeing it and did not know how grey his face was, and how lifeless.

It was shock to step across the threshold of the library and find everything unchanged. The chairs, the white bookcases, the rugs and curtains—even his pipe cleaners on the mantel behind the clock. He had left them there before he went away. He crossed the room and heard his own footsteps echoing. And knew that he would hear them as long as he lived.

Sophie followed him when she had hung his coat and hat in the hall closet. "There's some letters for you," she said.

"Some what?"

"There's some letters for you and some bills. They came while you were gone."

"Oh," James said.

"I put them on the table."

He looked at Sophie for the first time and saw that her eyes were red from weeping.

"I thought I'd tell you," she said.

"Yes."

"In case there might be something important."

"Yes, I'll look at them"—he realized suddenly why she looked so different. It was because she had no teeth. And with her mouth sunken in, Sophie had become an old woman—"after a while."

"I turned the spread back in your room so you can lay down if you want to, Mr. Morison."

"Thanks."

"Mrs. Hiller telegraphed from Decatur yesterday. She said to come and open the house this morning. And have the guest-room ready for Miss Blaney."

"For Miss Blaney? . . . Oh yes, I forgot about that. Or maybe they didn't tell me. It's all right, though. When is she coming?"

"The telegram didn't say. It just said to have the guest-room ready for her when she come. And Karl is going away."

"Where?"

"Why, didn't he tell you, Mr. Morison? He's going to Germany."

"Maybe he did. Yes, I guess so. When?"

"Right away. In a couple of days."

James put his hands over his eyes and felt the relief of darkness. His eyelids were cracked and hard. He had not slept for three nights. It did not seem likely that he would ever sleep again.

"You must be sure—" he said, slowly. "You must tell Karl to be sure and see me before he goes."

Sophie nodded. "He was here early this morning. I had him build a fire in the grate."

"What's that?"

"I had Karl build a fire in the grate."

"Oh."

"All you have to do is light a match to it."

"That's fine."

"When he comes I'll tell him you want to see him, Mr. Morison."

"If you will, Sophie."

James took the stack of letters with him and went over to the chaise-longue and sat down. *Mr. James B. Morison . . . Mr. James Morison, 553 W. Elm Street, Logan, Illinois . . . Mr. and Mrs. James B. Morison . . .* He read the envelopes again and again, without having the strength or the will to open them. *Mr. and Mrs. James B. Morison. . . .* When he closed his eyes for a moment and sank back, it was more than he could do to raise his head from the cushions.

"It's like being drunk," he said.

To his surprise, Sophie was still there and answered him.

"Once when I was a girl in the old country———"

James did not hear the end of her sentence. If he listened to Sophie, he would have to look at her. He would have to open his eyes.

"When I relax," he said, "when I sit too long in one place, it seems like I'm on the railway platform downtown. The train is coming in—the one we're going to take to Decatur. And there are people walking up and down the platform, waiting to get on."

"That's because you been sick . . . because you had the flu, Mr. Morison. You have to take good care of yourself."

"And I shove forward, knowing each time that if I'd

wait—but you see I didn't wait. That was the whole trouble. I was trying to get seats for us before the others got on. If I'd stepped back and let the others get on first, I'd have seen the interurban draw up alongside that train. On the other tracks.... The interurban had a parlor car that was almost empty. It would have been ever so much better to take that, don't you see? And turn our train tickets in later. That way we wouldn't have exposed ourselves. But we had suitcases and all the people were pushing us forward and the train was crowded already. There was nothing to do but go up the steps onto the train."

"That may be so, Mr. Morison," Sophie said. "But it don't help thinking about it. What's done can't be undone, I always say. The thing for you to do is lay there and be quiet and get some rest."

"Yes," James said, "you're quite right." And sprang up suddenly and began tearing the envelopes open, one after another. He read the letters while he walked back and forth between the fireplace and the windows—read them over and over without retaining what he read. Then he threw envelopes and letters upon the library table and stood perfectly still, pressing his shoulder against the mantel.

For two days now (ever since they came into his room at daybreak to tell him) he had been getting on that train. And there was no way, apparently, that he could stop.

II

The coffin was set in the bay window of the living-room, and James wanted to be alone. He wanted to have time to reconcile that fact with all other facts that he knew to be true and final. But almost as soon as the undertaker's men were out of the house, Wilfred appeared, bringing James's mother and Bunny.

Bunny was weeping.

"There," James said. "You mustn't take on so. You'll be sick." And struggled with the large buttons on the child's coat.

"I put his rubbers on," Wilfred said.

James looked at him earnestly.

"I say I put Bunny's rubbers on."

"Oh . . . much obliged to you."

"That's all right," Wilfred said. "Glad to do it, only I think I got them wrong foot to."

James nodded. If they'd only wait, let him be by himself for a while.

"Clara said to tell you she'd be over this evening right after supper."

"You must take your wraps off," James said. You mustn't stand here in the front hall." And wondered if his words sounded as desperate to them—and as foolish.

His mother unwound a heavy woolen scarf and looked at him with faded eyes.

"We must rejoice," she said before Wilfred could stop her. "Morison—" she said, "—Wilfred—I mean—*James,* we must rejoice! I keep saying that to myself. We must rejoice. She is gone to a better place like the Bible says. Where she'll always be happy. And we should all be that way, on her account. Even if we can't be happy for ourselves or for her poor motherless children. I said to Clara: *I can't get it out of my mind. It makes me think of your poor father,* I said. *Fourteen years ago your father died—in March. And it doesn't seem like any time at all. . . ."*

What happened night before last, James thought, would stay in his mind, too, whether he wanted to remember it or not. He was only two rooms down the hall at the hospital, and Thursday night, when she was worse, he lay awake all night, listening. The gas-light came through the transom and cut a rectangular hole in the ceiling. It was through that hole that the sound came to him. *Number seventeen*—a nurse said, so calmly that he wanted to get up and strike her across the mouth—*Number seventeen is having a hard time of it. . . .* As if he didn't hear and know all that was going on.

"*You don't know,* I said to Clara, *how many times I get down on my knees and thank God for taking him, for not letting him suffer."* James's mother allowed Wilfred to help with her coat. "Every few days he'd have a spell of terrific pain. Then we'd have to give him morphine. . . ."

When Bunny stopped weeping and turned to look at her, James separated him from his coat and mittens.

"Sophie is out in the kitchen," he said. "You'd better go out and say hello to her."

There was no point in a child's knowing these things.

"I'd been waiting for him to go," his mother said as they went into the library. "I'd been expecting it ever since he stopped eating. That's what carried him along, the doctor said—a good appetite. And he'd lost so much flesh. . . ."

With his eyes James begged Wilfred to take her away, but Wilfred was unable or unwilling. He sat down in the largest chair and crossed one knee over the other permanently.

"I don't think your father weighed much over a hundred and twenty or maybe a hundred and twenty-five, because there was nothing to him but skin and bones. Even so"— she turned and looked into Wilfred's face to make sure that he was listening—"even so, I didn't get much rest. It was hard lifting him, you know, and I stayed right in the same room with him for months. He'd rather lie there and suffer than call anybody. And I knew if I was near I'd hear him move. He'd have pain, you know, James. And then he'd take medicine and sleep."

James could not bear it any longer—to have her sitting there in a white wicker chair, nursing her grief.

"Did you have a nice time in Vandalia, Wilfred?"

"In Vandalia? Why, we didn't go."

"I thought you and Clara were going down there for Thanksgiving."

"We did intend to. But we'd have had to go on the train, and with so much sickness about, we were afraid to risk it. But I thought Clara told you all that when you called up about the boys?"

"The boys? Yes, I guess she did. I'd forgotten about it. Have they been all right? And behaved themselves?"

"Robert's been sick."

"Oh . . . is that so?"

"Yes, Robert's been a sick boy," his mother said. "A mighty sick boy!"

James lowered himself into the chaise-longue until his head struck the pillows.

"Yesterday morning," Wilfred said, "things were pretty upset after you called, and Robert got up out of bed before he was supposed to. Today, the doctor said. But Clara got in touch with him during the forenoon and he said it was all right if Robert didn't have any temperature. And he didn't—this was yesterday—so I guess it *will* be. He has to keep quiet, of course."

James caught a glimpse of a pocket knife: Wilfred was going to pare his finger nails.

"He didn't seem to take it as hard as Bunny did. But then I always thought Bunny showed his mother more affection." Wilfred closed the knife blade with a sigh. "Clara was going to tell you but in case she forgets—if you want to bring the baby home after the funeral, we'd be only too glad to take it and look after it for you."

James sat up. "I don't know." He steadied himself carefully with his hands. "They're going to keep the baby at the hospital for a while. The baby's all right, I guess, but they want to keep it there. And after that I don't know exactly what I want to do. I haven't had time to think about it."

The front door opened while James was speaking.

"We want to be of help," Wilfred said, "in any way that we possibly can."

"That's very kind of you."

"Until you get straightened around," Wilfred said.

Irene appeared in a draught of cold air. Her blue coat was half unbuttoned. She spoke to each of them.

Then gravely, without any expression on her face, she made her way around Wilfred's feet and drew the curtains together across the library windows. With grateful eyes James followed her. She turned on the table lamp, and in the blue bowl on the mantel found matches to light the fire. When Bunny came in, the room was bright and habitable.

She smiled at him. "You know your agate," she said, and took the blue bowl down from the mantel. "The yellow agate that you told me was lost? Well I've found it."

Bunny looked at her quietly.

"Here it is."

"Irene," Bunny said, "it's so terrible here!" And buried his face in the lining of her coat.

Irene's smile went all to pieces. She knelt down and put her arms about him. "Everything's going to be all right," she said. "Only you mustn't cry, do you hear? You mustn't cry."

Bunny dried his face with the back of his hand, and took the bowl and the yellow agate.

"I know," he said, and sat down on the floor to play.

Irene stood looking at him thoughtfully, until her eyes were no longer blurred. Then she turned to James and said, "When's Robert coming home?"

"He isn't, I guess."

"Why not?"

"He's been sick."

"I know he has. I just came from there."

"Clara doesn't think Robert ought to come home," Wilfred began. "He wasn't even supposed to———"

Irene interrupted him. "I called Dr. Macgregor and he said he'd seen Robert early this morning, and that it was all right if we wanted to bring him home. . . . Clara wouldn't listen, James. I told her . . . I told her everything Dr. Macgregor said. But she said Robert was going to stay there just the same. . . . I left him sitting in a chair by the front window with his rubbers on."

"If Clara doesn't think he ought to come home," James said, "perhaps it would be just as well to——"

"Don't you *want* him here?"

"Certainly."

"Well, do you mind if I call and tell her that?"

James shut his eyes.

"Tell her anything you like."

He would have shut his mind, too, if it had been possible. He was very tired. And weak. And there was no reason why they could not make these arrangements among themselves.

From what Wilfred was saying—a word now and then, or a phrase—James gathered that the churches had been closed on account of the epidemic. But they were soon to be opened again. As for the epidemic, Wilfred said, that was on the wane. No new cases had been reported yesterday or the day before.

Against his will James listened and heard Irene's voice locked in argument.

"I know, Clara, but the doctor says it's all right . . . yes. . . . Yes, James wants him here. . . ."

They had traced the epidemic, Wilfred said, to the original source and found that it was brought to this country in German submarines.

"Yes. . . . Yes, Clara. . . . Yes, I know!"

James looked at Irene uneasily. There was no color in her face—none whatever.

"Yes," she said, very slowly. "Yes ... yes ..." And gave herself over to brilliant unreasonable laughter that didn't stop when it should have, but went on and on into the mouthpiece of the telephone.

III

It was Wilfred who took the receiver out of Irene's hand and told Clara to have the boy ready in fifteen minutes. For that James would be grateful always. Ethel came in from the late afternoon train and went upstairs right away to look after Irene. When his mother and Wilfred had gone, James stood with his back to the fire until the little brass clock on the mantel tick-tick-tick-ticked itself out of existence and the room grew quiet around him.

At five-thirty Robert came in. He had a book under one arm and a box of soldiers under the other, and he limped more noticeably than usual. When Robert was tired, he did not care how he walked, but led with his good leg, in spite of all that James had told him, and dragged his artificial leg behind.

Robert shook hands with his father solemnly and put the soldiers and the book on the library table. Then he went over to the windows and sat down.

James could not help thinking (for the thousandth time, perhaps) that it was a great pity Robert had to have his leg cut off. There was no doubt but that Robert would have made an athlete—a real athlete—if he'd had the chance.

"How are you feeling, son?"

"All right," Robert said.

"Kind of wabbly?"

"Yes."

"So am I. We'll have to be careful for a while. Both of us."

Their eyes met and they agreed that there was something in the house which was not to be talked about. The best and possibly the only solution, so far as James could see, was for Clara to take the baby. And the boys, too. For he couldn't keep the house going—that was certain. He'd have to store what furniture he wanted. That wasn't much. He had never cared for antiques the way Elizabeth did. And sell all the rest. Sell the house, too, for what he could get.

Wilfred did not offer to take the boys, but it would be all right, probably. James would give Clara so much a month for boarding them and for their clothes—because he would not have Wilfred or anybody else paying for the support of his children. And he'd get a room near by. Clara's wasn't the kind of home they were used to, perhaps. But it would do until such time as he was able to make a better arrangement.

In the long run it was a mistake to have children. James did not understand them. He never knew what was going on in their minds. But that was Elizabeth's doing, after all. It was she who had wanted them.

There were some men who had a natural way with children. Tom Macgregor, for instance. They came to him in a room full of people. When Bunny and Robert were little, they would come to their father sometimes to have cigar smoke blown into their ears. Bunny did still, when he had the earache. But not very often. If they had been girls it might have been different. James felt more at ease with little girls. They came and sat on his lap and played with his watch-fob. And they seemed to like very much the riddles he told them. Robert and Bunny were forever arguing, contending with each other like Cain and Abel. So that it was mostly a matter of keeping them separated and making each one play with his own toys.

And without her . . . James went into the front hall and stared for a long time at the umbrella-stand. Without Elizabeth it was more than he could manage.

On the second trip into the front hall he went through the white columns and into the living-room. Then into the library by the door at the farther end. If he could only go back, if he could remember everything during the last ten days, why then he might—it was foolish of course, but the same idea occurred to him over and over—he might be able to change what had already happened.

In his whole life he had never been sick before—not seriously. And being sick, he could not make people do the things he wanted them to. There was no way. They would not even let him get up and go into her room at the hospital and see her—except that once, late Wednesday afternoon.

The nurse brought a chair for him and made him sit some distance away from the bed. Elizabeth was better, she said. But he could not help seeing how difficult it was for her to breathe. It seemed to take all her strength for that. When she looked at him, when she spoke to him, his hands trembled violently and there was nothing that he could think of to say.

He sat and looked at her hair that was spread out over

the pillow, and remembered the first time he had ever seen her. She was driving a pony cart on Tremont Street and she had two little girls in the cart with her and the little girls wore big blue hair-ribbons.

That in turn reminded James of something else— something that he had never quite forgotten. That matter of Bunny and the pony. Robert had several of them in succession, and when Bunny was old enough he wanted one, too. It was only natural. But they had torn down the barn and replaced it with a garage by that time. So there was nowhere to keep a pony, and they would have had to pay Karl or somebody to look after it. All things considered, it would have been too much expense. When Bunny's birthday came along, without saying anything to Elizabeth he took Bunny down to the livery-stable and had them bring out a colt that wasn't yet weaned from its mother. Then he said *There's your pony, son. Lead it home.* Of course the colt reared up on its hind legs, and Bunny tugged and yanked until he became frightened. Then he began to cry, and the colt cried, and all the men came out of the barber shop to laugh at them. So he took the halter out of Bunny's hands, and the colt was led back to the stable.

When he got home and told Elizabeth, there was the devil to pay. She wouldn't speak to him or look at him or let him come near her. It was the first time he had ever seen her that way, and it scared him. Because he hadn't meant to do anything wrong. He simply wanted to cure Bunny of all desire for a pony—which he did. But Elizabeth wouldn't listen to him. He tried to explain to her how it was, but she said *James, how could you?* with Bunny right there, listening. So he told her to put skirts on the boy, for Christ's sake, and be done with it.

He saw afterward that he had been in the wrong, but there never seemed to be any way that he could mention it. Not without bringing up the whole business all over again.

And at the hospital when he leaned forward to tell her how he felt (he had been wrong, of course; he never should have talked to her like that) the nurse came in. The nurse had the baby with her, wrapped in a white blanket. And Elizabeth smiled her slow smile and said, *Look, James, another peeing boy. . . .*

IV

Each time that James passed through the living-room he was careful to look at the sofa or the French windows which led into the back part of the house. Nevertheless, he felt drawn, pulled toward the bay window, until at last he could get no farther. The coffin was grey with silver handles. And if it were really Elizabeth, James thought—if he should see Elizabeth when he stepped up to it (her dark hair and her forehead and the slope of her throat)—he did not know what he would do.

He stood there a few feet away, with his heart racing wildly like a machine. And Sophie had to call him twice to dinner before he understood.

Ethel and the boys were waiting for him in the dining-room.

"Would you like me to serve, James?" she said.

James looked at her in bewilderment. She pronounced her words precisely the way a school-teacher would.

"I always do the serving," he said.

"Yes, but I thought that perhaps if you weren't feeling well——"

"I'm all right," James said. "I'm quite all right."

They sat down together—Ethel in Elizabeth's place at the end of the table. When James was with her he found himself on guard for fear that he would make some mistake in his English. He spoke as well as the average person, he supposed. As well as anyone ought to speak. But Ethel had gone East to school. She had gone to Bryn Mawr and she never seemed to want to marry. When she was younger and before her hair turned grey, she was attractive enough. James knew of several men that she could have had. But she was too well educated for a woman and she didn't want any of them.

"For Miss Blaney," he said. And when Sophie took the plate that he handed her, James noticed that she was self-conscious on account of her teeth.

"How much are they going to cost, Sophie?" he said when she returned to his end of the table.

"What, Mr. Morison?"

"Your teeth."

"I don't know, exactly," she said, with the colour mounting upward into her face. "About fifty dollars." She set Bunny's plate in front of him. "But if I'd known how much it would take, I don't guess I'd of had them out. But they were hurting me so, night and day——"

"You did the right thing, I'm sure," Ethel said. "And Robert needs more water."

James wondered if he had said something that he shouldn't have, if he had said something unkind. "When the time comes to get your new teeth, let me know, Sophie. I might be able to help you with them." He took up the carving-knife and began sharpening it. And Sophie beside him pulled the hem out of her apron in gratitude.

When Robert had been served, she returned once more to the head of the table.

"That Karl is here . . ."

James unfolded his napkin.

"Tell him I'll be out as soon as we're through dinner," he said.

Sophie disappeared through the swinging doors, and James took up his knife and fork. He found, strangely, that he could not eat. When he tried, the food turned solid in his throat and would not go down. There was nothing to do but sit with his plate untouched before him, and watch his sons, who were still too young to confuse grief with a good appetite.

When Robert passed things it was always without speaking and without looking up—as if the interruption were barely tolerable. With Bunny it seemed to be largely a matter of making him hear, for he ate with his eyes on some object (the corner of a dish) and there was no telling where his mind was.

"How is Irene?" James said.

"Resting. I put cold cloths on her head. That's about all anybody can do, you know, after she's had one of those spells."

When Ethel was a little girl, Elizabeth had said, she could not bear to get dirt on her clean white stockings.

Bunny was recalled from wherever it was that he had been.

"Is it true, Aunt Eth— Is it true that Irene married Uncle Boyd Hiller for his money?"

The silence was so immediate and so intense that James

could hear the big clock ticking sullenly in the front hall, two rooms away. "No, son, it isn't true——" and feel his jaw relax. "You mustn't say things like that, do you hear?"

Bunny nodded, and would have gone on eating, James thought, if Ethel had not leaned forward in her chair with hard bright eyes.

"Who told you that, Bunny?"

"It's something he's made up," James said.

"I didn't, either, make it up—it's what Grandmother Morison told Amanda Matthews."

Robert put his fork down with a clatter.

"Who is Amanda Matthews?"

"She's a girl in Aunt Clara's Sunday-school class that was at Aunt Clara's house night before last."

James saw that Ethel was smiling at him queerly.

"Well, however it was," she said, "you misunderstood. Your grandmother wouldn't say such a thing."

If she were only a man, James thought.

"But she did, Aunt Eth. She said there was somebody else that Irene wanted to marry but Grandmother Blaney kept after her night and day, saying what a fine young man Uncle Boyd was, because he had been to Princeton and——"

"Bunny, that's enough."

The interurban was drawing alongside the train, on the other tracks. And James had to wait for a minute before he could go on speaking.

"Suppose you tell us, son, what you were doing all this time?"

"He was on the couch," Robert volunteered, "in the sitting-room, pretending like he was asleep."

"When I want information from you, Robert, I'll ask for it. . . . Go up to your room now, both of you."

They had made trouble enough for one evening—trouble that would last for months and months, and when Irene found out about it, breed more and more trouble.

"Well," he said, "what are you waiting for?"

As soon as they had gone—Robert looking injured and Bunny in tears again—James set about to deal with the image that obsessed him. With so much sickness, with the epidemic everywhere it stood to reason that someone with influenza might have been on that interurban, too. They might have been exposed to influenza there, just as they were on the crowded train. And what point was there in torturing himself like this? What good did it do?

"You might at least have waited," Ethel said from the other end of the table. "You might have let them stay and have their dessert."

James gripped the edge of his chair with both hands and said very quietly, "They're my children, Ethel, and I'll do with them as I think best."

V

Wilfred returned with Clara almost immediately after dinner.

"It doesn't seem possible," Clara said. "I say it just doesn't seem possible! She was so young, and with so much to live for!"

James had no idea what to say, or what was expected of him. But as the evening progressed, more and more people came—Lyman and Amelia Shepherd, Maud Ahrens, the Hinkleys, the McIntyres, the Lloyds—until the library was filled with them. And by that time James had adjusted his mind to the rhetoric of the occasion. What bewildered him was not the set phrases, and not the repetition, but the fact that they were sincerely spoken. *Such a loss,* people said to him with tears in their eyes. *So tragic that she should have to be taken....* Then because there were so many that they could not all talk to him, they fell back upon one another politely, as if that were why they had come. They discussed the peace terms and the price of meat. They talked about the weather, which was severe for December—only the beginning, one might say, of the cold months.

James tried to take a suitable interest in the conversation, but he could not keep from glancing up when each new person came into the room, and strange ideas ran through his head. It seemed to him that except for an unwillingness to interrupt one another, people acted very much as if they had come here to a party. The house had taken possession of them—Elizabeth's house—and they were having a good time.

Clara and Wilfred went home, and then the Shepherds, and then the McIntyres, almost without James's noticing it. The air grew heavy with smoke. And after a while he discovered that it was not necessary for him even to seem to be listening. He was glad when nine o'clock came and one by one they stood up to leave—all except young Johnston, who had brought his mail out to him from the office and did not know apparently how to go home.

While Johnston talked in his thin bookkeeper's voice about the office and about the adjustment of a certain loss, James sat with his hand over his left side. It was something that he had never thought about until now, and there was no reason why it should occur to him particularly, except that he felt very wide awake after not having slept for days and days. But the strange thing was that he could hear his own heart ticking under his vest—keeping time there like a clock.

"I've come down from Chicago," a voice said—an unmistakable voice. James sprang up and went to the front hall, but he was too late. Boyd Hiller was there. He was inside the door, talking to Ethel, and there was that same tired handsomeness about him. He had not changed, except that it seemed to be an effort for him to carry himself so well. As Ethel started up the stairs, he turned and saw James in the doorway.

"Good evening," he said.

Once upon a time James met Boyd Hiller with Robert unconscious in his arms. And later (years later) James had slammed the front door in his face. The extreme courtesy of Boyd's manner implied that he remembered both incidents.

In any family, James thought, it was like that. Nothing was ever forgotten.

There were no chairs in the front hall—only a sofa beside the window. Both men remained standing. When the tension became uncomfortable, James said, "Are you living in Chicago now?"

"For a short while."

Boyd cleared his throat.

"New York is my headquarters, though, and has been the last two years. I'm on the stock exchange."

"That must be interesting," James said, and thought grimly of the time Boyd put soap in the minnow-bucket.

"You get used to it."

"Yes, I suppose."

Irene was coming down the stairs in a green kimono.

"You get used to anything," James said.

When Irene reached the bottom step, she waited there. Boyd started toward her with years of unhappiness in his eyes.

"I didn't know," he said, and stopped at the edge of the dark red rug. "I didn't know until just now when I came up the walk. I can't tell you how shocked and how sorry I am!"

Irene stepped down and shook hands with him gravely. "You've been sick," she said.

Boyd nodded.

"Flu?"

"It was a light case. When I was able to go back to the hotel I found your note, and here I am."

James understood now why Irene had gone off to Chicago. It was written on her face plainly, for anyone to see. She would return to Boyd Hiller and run through that whole unhappy business all over again. If they wanted to do that, James thought, it was all right with him. But he turned away without a word to either of them.

VI

The flowers in Irene's kimono were almost but not quite the colour of her hair. And James decided that no matter what people said, it was not money. Irene had not married Boyd for that, nor would she go back to him for any such reason. There was no telling how she felt about Boyd now, but at one time, before they began quarrelling so, she had been fond of him. On her wedding day she broke a mirror and perhaps it was that which ruined their marriage—bad luck as much as anything.

Somehow it was impossible to think of her leading a calm, ordinary life. Wherever Irene was, there was excitement. Now when she gathered the folds of her kimono and leaned toward the fire, her hair glittered. Her hair gave off light.

"I think we know sometimes what is going to happen to us," she said. "I remember things that didn't seem to have any meaning till now, and they fit. . . . We were upstairs, James, in your bedroom, and Elizabeth was doing her hair. I was sitting on the bed, watching her, and all of a sudden it occurred to me how complicated it was. And I told her about it, and she laughed and said that nobody would be able to do it for her when she was dead. . . . I said for her not to talk like that because it was wrong and silly and there was no telling how long anybody would live. But she took the hairpins out of her mouth and said, *Within three years.*"

James got up out of his chair and began to walk. He could not and would not believe what Irene was saying. With other people Elizabeth had a front—an odd way of covering up her feelings or of disguising them. No one had any idea, for instance, how deeply she felt about Robert's accident. She stayed in the bedroom with him for hours at a time, entertaining him and helping him play with the soldiers Irene brought—all as if nothing were the matter. And neither Robert nor anyone else knew that at night she turned into his arms and wept.

He could not believe that in these later years she had lain awake at his side night after night, planning and arranging things for a time when she would not be here. If her life had been overshadowed by the anticipation of dying, he would have known it. She could not have kept it from him.

"It's the kind of thing that people remember," he said, "after some one is dead. You might never have thought anything more about it except for that. It's like any common superstition—thirteen at the table or a dog howling or a bird in the house."

"You know there was one," Irene said. "There was a bird in Bunny's room while he was sick. It was the day Karl took down the screens. I didn't tell you afterward because I knew it would worry you— Not the bird, but something that it was too late to do anything about. It was my fault, really. But

Elizabeth sent Robert for a broom. Then in our excitement we both forgot and went into the room where Bunny was. So that when Robert came back he saw her sitting on the edge of Bunny's bed.... And ever since, he's been thinking that if anything happened to his mother, he'd be responsible. You didn't know that, did you, James? ... And tonight when they came upstairs, I went in to see them. They were both pretty miserable because they had been sent from the table, so I talked to them for a while about their mother—until Robert broke down and told me what was on his mind. You have to watch him, James, and talk with him more than you do, and find out what there is back of what he's saying. Because he's at the age to get notions.... I explained to him that people caught the flu within three days after they were exposed to it. What he was worrying about happened a long time before his mother took sick. I don't know whether he believed me or not. Perhaps he did. But in the morning I'll have Dr. Macgregor come and talk to him. It's things like that—don't you see? Now that there isn't anybody to keep an eye on him ... And each of us has his private nightmare. Robert isn't the only one."

James looked at her oddly to see whether by some mischance she knew about the interurban.

"I keep remembering," she said, "how selfish I was those last weeks—always thinking about Boyd and whether I could bring myself to go back to him. And I sort of took what was happening to her for granted. That was the way it always was. As a person, James, I could never hold a candle to her. Nobody could.... I remember we went, the two of us, to see a woman who had cooked for my mother, and who was very sick. She lived in an old house on Tenth Street, and such a place.... I gathered my skirts around me so as not to touch the furniture or the children. Elizabeth was every bit as much dressed up as I was, but nobody would have known from the way she acted that there was anything wrong. . . . She went over to the bed where the woman lay, and sat down, and took her hand."

James sighed. He had been along with them that day. It was just after Elizabeth and he were married. He had gone into the dirty ramshackle house on Tenth Street when they did. But Irene didn't care whether he knew it or not. She was talking about Elizabeth for the pain it caused her.

"And there's something else, James . . . something I have to tell you. At the last when she was so terribly sick she motioned with her hand. As if she wanted to write. I went over to her and said *Tell me what it is you want done, Bess, and I'll do it . . .*"

James got up and went to the window and threw it wide open. And small white papers that he had stuffed into the cracks to keep the draught out were scattered across the room.

"*It's about my baby,* she said. *I don't want the Morisons to have my baby.*"

The air was not as cold as James had expected, but dark and full of snow.

VII

When James opened the door from the butler's pantry into the kitchen, he found only darkness. It was no more than reasonable, he told himself, that Karl should have got tired waiting and gone home. For it was after eleven, and he promised to come out as soon as dinner was over.

The scene at the table had driven everything else out of his mind. And people began coming. . . . There was no need to say that to Ethel. He should have known better. But if there was one thing that he could not stand, it was having somebody step in and tell him how to run his affairs. . . . He groped his way past the table to the sink. The kitchen was bare and in complete order as Sophie had left it. James was about to turn and go back to the front part of the house when he heard scratching outside, and knew why it was that he had come here.

When he opened the door, there were two eyes shining at him out of the darkness. Old John hobbled across the sill.

"Did they forget you, old fellow?" James said.

The dog looked at him reproachfully.

It was beginning, James thought to himself—the final and complete disintegration of his house. Wherever he turned he would find it. Elizabeth was gone, and things would not be done which should be done. . . . He put his face down and buried it (for there was no one here to see him) in the cold fur of the dog's side. Old John whined softly.

Why, James thought, why am I doing this? And straightened up immediately and made the dog comfortable beside the stove. Then he turned the light out and went back the way he had come—through the butler's pantry and the dining-room and around the library to the front hall. Mr. Koenig had come over from next door, and he was in the library. And on the fifth step of the stairs James paused, remembering why people sat up all night with the dead.

Then he went on up the stairs and across the upstairs hall to the bedroom which Elizabeth and he had shared. And saw her dresses hanging in the closet, and was struck blind and almost senseless. When he could, he shut the closet door quickly, and pressed his forehead into the long cool mirror which was on the other side.

Satin
and lace
and brown velvet
and the faint odor of violets

—That was all which was left to him of his love. In anger then (for she could have sent some word to him and she had not) he went about the room picking up her brush or her ivory mirror or the tiny bottle of smelling-salts, and putting them down again. One after another he opened drawers, gathering small intimate things—hairpins, sachet-bags, a sponge soaked in powder, a score-card, a tassel, a string of amber beads—and made a pile of them on the dresser. For she had put him aside, he said to himself, *casually* with her life.

The weakness which was in his shoulders went down through his hips to his knees. He stood in the centre of the room, rocking forward and back; and in his ears heard that terrible last hour of her breathing. . . . He would sell the house, he thought over and over like a lesson to be memorized. A lesson that he would recite tomorrow when the time came. And Clara could take the children since she wanted them. And everything else—Elizabeth's clothes, her amethysts and pearls (he dumped them out on the dresser), her smallest articles he would give to Ethel, to Irene, to Sophie, to anybody with the kindness and mercy to have them. Because she was gone now. And when he had finished, there would be no trace of her anywhere. No one would know there had ever been such a person, he said to himself. And turned to the doorway, and saw Bunny staring at him with Elizabeth's frightened eyes.

VIII

The wind had fallen. There was an inch of snow on the front walk and more of it coming down steadily on James's coat sleeve and on his gloved hands and whirling in a silent frenzy about the street lamp. The crotches of trees were white with it, and each separate branch outlined. When James looked up he could see the night sky all dark, and the moist snow dropping into his face, into his open mouth.

He had come down the stairs and out of the house as he had done every day of his life, but with this difference—he was not going back. He would not enter that empty house again. Here on the sidewalk (with snow falling so thick that a man ten feet away would hardly know him) he was alone.

He turned to the left, as the snow turned, and walked past the first house, which was the Koenigs', and past the second, which was the Mitchells', and the third. . . . They were all asleep in their beds, with no knowledge of him, or that he was here on the sidewalk looking at their darkened houses.

The house of Elizabeth's father was on the other side of

the street and occupied by strangers. He had nothing to fear from it. . . . He and Elizabeth lived there when they were first married, with her father and mother and with Irene. Elizabeth's father read Ingersoll and questioned every accepted idea on religion and morality, so that it was an education for a young man to be with him. But during his last illness he changed his mind about things, and he stopped questioning. *It's like this, James,* he would say. *There's the earth—the continents and the seas, and the moon revolving around the earth, and the sun beyond that, and all the constellations. And beyond the constellations are stars without number or name, millions of them, whirling in space. You know that, James, without my telling you.* . . . But for time or the passage of time they might be there now, talking—James himself, only younger, and an old man dying of a horrible infection in his head.

James leaned against a tree. The snow was all about him like a curtain. And he could almost believe that they were still in that house across the street. *Somebody made it—some power—according to laws that can't be changed or added to. . . . The same now as they were thousands of years ago. . . . It's got to be like that. Otherwise it wouldn't work. . . .*

When James put both hands behind him, he felt the rough bark of the tree through his leather gloves. His fingers were getting cold and stiff.

"But to what purpose?" he said aloud, and hearing the words, he lost their meaning and all connection with what had gone before.

He knew only that there was frozen ground under his feet, and that the trees he saw were real and he could by moving out of his path touch them. The snow dropping out of the sky did not turn when he turned or make any concession to his needs, but only to his existence. The snow fell on his shoulders and on the brim of his hat and it stayed there and melted. He was real. That was all he knew.

He was here in this night, walking across the corner of a yard, over a sidewalk, down a vacant street. When he stopped to get his bearings, he saw that without knowing it he had turned up the alley. There were deep frozen ruts along each side of the road, and telephone poles one after another leaning against the sky. Ahead of him he heard wheels creaking and the placing (muffled and delicate) of hoofs. The placing of hoofs on snow. And knew suddenly that it was all a mistake . . . everything that he had thought and done this day.

He was alive, that was the trouble. He was caught up in his own living and breathing and there was no way possible for him to get out. Elizabeth knew that, and she had come after him in the pony cart. She had come to take him home.

He was glad. He was immensely excited. His hands shook and his knees. He began to run along the alley, stumbling and falling and picking himself up again. He ran until he was stopped by the lean shape of a horse, and a wagon with a lantern on it. The lantern shone upward into a man's face that was thin and patient and crazy.

With the last of his strength gone out of him, James leaned against the firm lattice-work of his own back fence.

IX

James awoke late into a room that was bright with the morning sun. On the dresser were Elizabeth's things lying in a heap as he had left them. When he looked outside the snow blinded him. He stretched his legs under the covers until they touched the foot of the bed, and wondered how many mornings of his life he had lain here—awake and watching the curtains blow in from the open window. And whether the lightness he felt inside him was grief. Or if he would ever be capable of any emotion again.

Slowly and with care he bathed and shaved and dressed himself in clean clothes. He staggered slightly when he went from the closet to the dresser to comb his hair. But his head was clear, and when he put his hands to his eyelids, they no longer felt cracked and hard. . . . There were formalities and customs, there was the funeral to be got through with somehow this day.

Ethel was in the guest-room, making her bed. He lingered at the door until she noticed him.

"You look rested, James," she said. "Did you sleep?"

He looked into her eyes and saw nothing but kindness there—kindness and a veiled sympathy.

"Yes, I think I did."

"That's what you needed more than anything else."

For the first time it occurred to him that Ethel might keep from Irene what Bunny said last night at the table— that she had no intention of telling her.

"Thank you," he said, and hoped that she would understand what for.

"Irene is off on some errand. With Boyd, I think. But your mother is here and Clara, too. You'll find them in the sewing-room."

At the head of the stairs James listened and heard their voices. They were arguing over certain tags which had come with the flowers—one from the men in his office and the other from Bunny's class at school.

"If you'd only waited," Clara was saying. "If you'd only let *me* open them . . ."

James started down. On the landing he met Robert and Tom Macgregor. Robert held a medical journal tightly under one arm.

"The boy's all right, James. Only he's a trifle stick-headed like his father."

James stepped aside to let them go up the stairs.

"Take it easy, son," he said.

Though it was nearly ten o'clock, there was no one in the front hall or the living room or the library. And James's place was still set at the dining-room table. He went on to the kitchen, which was warm and bright. Karl sat with his overcoat on and the sweat running down his face. Bunny was beside him at the kitchen table. And Sophie, rattling the breakfast dishes, created such a cheerful noise that none of them heard James, or knew that he was there.

Bunny was making a wreath of ferns. And it was hardly the thing, James thought. Bunny ought not to be making a game of flowers that had been sent to his mother's funeral. As James started forward he could have sworn, almost, that he felt a slight pressure on his arm. And he turned, in spite of himself—in spite of the fact that he knew positively no one was there.

X

With his coffee James smoked a cigarette—the first since he had been sick. Irene came in before he had finished.

"I've been out driving," she said, and sat down beside him at the dining-room table.

"With Boyd?"

"Yes. Did Ethel tell you?" Irene unbuttoned her left glove and then buttoned it again. "I've made up my mind, James—or rather I've had it made up for me. Boyd has to live in New York and I'd have to live there, too, it seems, if I went back to him."

"What are you going to do, then?"

"Stay here and help you look after the children."

From her expression it was impossible to tell whether the choice had been easy.

"Boyd is fonder of little Agnes than he is of me. I don't think he knows that, but he is. After he carried her off that time, I knew it. And I was afraid to have him see her. But I don't feel like that any more. He's so frightfully lonely. And there's no reason why he shouldn't have her part of the year. If I could be sure that I might be a different person, or that he could—but what has happened once can happen again. No matter what it is or how hard you try to avoid it. And where the going hasn't been too good it seems better not to double back on my own trail."

"No," James said, "I suppose not."

He put out his right hand and produced a chord—G, D flat, and F—on the dining-room table. Then he took a final drag at his cigarette.

"About the children, Irene—the main thing is to provide a home for them. I know that's what Elizabeth would want me to do."

"Yes, James, but it won't be easy. . . . I wasn't sure that it could be done. Bunny was so close to his mother, you know. She seemed almost to be aware of every breath he took. And when they were in the same room together, he was always turning his face toward her. Last night when he came in and looked at me that way, I felt that there was nothing to be done—nothing that you or I or anyone else could do for him. But this morning it's entirely different. The house is so bright, James, and so full of sunlight."

James leaned forward in his chair.

"I came in through the kitchen just now," Irene said, "and when I saw Bunny making wreaths, I knew somehow——"

Don't say it, James implored silently. *Don't say it!*

"——I knew that there was a chance that things might work out all right."

XI

While the man from the undertaker's went back for another
load of chairs, there was time for James to walk—to make
the circuit from the library out into the front hall, then
through the living-room, which was filled with flowers, and
into the library again.

James would have preferred to walk alone, but Robert
stood waiting at the foot of the stairs and James did not
have the heart to refuse him. Robert was freed from his
mistake. It was evident from the way he walked. Neither
Robert nor anyone else was responsible for Elizabeth's
death. It was what people intended to do that counted—
not what came about because of anything they did. James
saw that, clearly. And he saw that his life was like all other
lives. It had the same function. And it differed from them
only in shape—as one salt-cellar is different from another.
Or one knife-blade. What happened to him had happened
before. And it could happen again, more than once. Probably some one would lie awake all night in that very same
hospital feeling his lungs contract and expand, contract,

expand—until the whole of him was limited to the one effort of breathing.... But it would not be on account of Elizabeth, who was dying of pneumonia two rooms down the hall.

He would have liked to explain this to Robert. And about the rectangle of light on the ceiling above his bed. And also about the interurban, which no longer bothered him. It would be years probably before he could make Robert understand what happened when he met Crazy Jake collecting tin cans at midnight. But there was comfort at least in Robert's company, and in resting his arm on Robert's shoulders. Robert belonged to him. James could feel that in the way they walked together. They were of the same blood.

When he was Robert's age his father and mother went South and took him with them, for the winter. They rented a farmhouse on the side of a hill overlooking a Confederate cemetery. And he had no one to play with, being a Northerner, and he wanted to go home.

James remembered that winter, though of all the rest of his boyhood there was almost nothing left to him. The remembrance of a cellar door that sloped and could be used for hiding. A mulberry tree and the smell of harness, and brown stain of walnuts on his hands.... Even these things could not be shared with Robert, who was growing up in a later and more complicated world.

When James changed the direction of their walking, it brought them straight toward the coffin. They stepped up to it, together, and it was not as James had expected. He was not in the least afraid with Robert beside him. He stood looking down at Elizabeth's hands, which were folded irrevocably about a bunch of purple violets. He had not known that anything could be so white as they were—and so intensely quiet now with the life, with the identifying soul gone out of them.

They would not have been that way, he felt, if he had not been doing what she wanted him to do. For it was Elizabeth who had determined the shape that his life should take, from the very first moment that he saw her. And she had altered that shape daily by the sound of her voice, and by her hair, and by her eyes which were so large and dark. And by her wisdom and by her love.

"You won't forget your mother, will you, Robert?" he said. And with wonder clinging to him (for it had been a revelation: neither he nor anyone else had known that his life was going to be like this) he moved away from the coffin.

A NOTE ON THE TYPE

The principal text of this Modern Library edition
was set in a digitized version of Janson,
a typeface that dates from about 1690 and was cut by Nicholas Kis,
a Hungarian working in Amsterdam. The original matrices have
survived and are held by the Stempel foundry in Germany.
Hermann Zapf redesigned some of the weights and sizes for Stempel,
basing his revisions on the original design.